C000297874

Satin

(Silk and Thorne #2)

by

L. K. RAYNE

A rose's rarest essence lives in the thorn.
-    Rumi

Circumstances

"Maybe he just didn't have a condom," April suggested.

I placed a few slices of bulgogi from the grill plate into her metal rice bowl, hoping that the more she ate, the less she would try to make me feel better by making outlandish proposals. It wasn't that I didn't appreciate her support, but I seriously doubted there was anything April could say to save my dignity.

April nodded her thanks and gingerly plucked a piece of lettuce from the heap sitting in a plastic basket on the table.

"The sane thing to do in that situation would have been to tell me he needed to make a run to the pharmacy, or I don't know…" I picked up the next plate of raw meat, some kind of pork, and slid the entire contents onto the sizzling grill top with my chopsticks. "April, it wasn't the condom."

"I know, I know, it was just a suggestion," April said. She wrapped the cooked bulgogi with lettuce, added some bean sauce and a slice of garlic before stuffing it into her mouth and munching ponderously.

It made her look a bit like a chipmunk. A Korean Barbeque eating chipmunk.

She swallowed, then reached for another piece of lettuce. "Maybe he's gay?" she offered, giving me a shocked scandalous look.

I groaned. Her suggestion brought the memory to the forefront of my mind. I could vividly remember the way he'd kissed me, the way he'd grabbed my hips, the way he'd... gotten hard. "If Ethan's gay, then he's the best undiscovered acting talent in Los Angeles since... since..."

"Since Harrison Ford?" April offered.

I nodded. "Exactly." It seemed like April was finally reaching the conclusion that her suggestions were nuts.

April finished wrestling the food down into her belly, then sat up suddenly. "You're gonna burn the samgyeopsal!"

I quickly grabbed my tongs and aimed it as the grill, my eyes darting between the different meats. "Which one is the sam...sanyup..."

"Samgyeopsal!" April waved her chopsticks at the grill. "Obviously that one! The thick one!" She pointed with her chopsticks. "The server even said the names out loud as she placed them on the table."

"I just eat whatever you order," I said, pushing the rectangular slices of meat to the edge of the grill where they would be safe. "We don't come regularly enough for me to remember all the names."

"Well, remember them now, sheesh! It's *so* good, how can you *not* want to remember?" She suddenly switched her demeanor, leaning toward me in a conspiratory manner, tilting her head just so, then flicking her eyebrows up and down. "Remember them like Ethan remembered you."

Her quick changes in demeanor always made me laugh, but I could only respond with a reserved smile this time. I wasn't one to turn up my nose at marinated grilled meat, but the only reason we were even at this smoke filled restaurant in Koreatown was because Ethan remembered me. I couldn't help huffing a bit as I saved the remaining samgyeopsal from disaster.

"It's really a lot simpler than you're making it out to be. We ran into each other at a charity ball. I spilled water onto his crotch. We had a little too much to drink…one thing led to another and…and then he realized how big of a liability it could be for someone in his position to hook up with a random woman he remembered from when he was a kid."

"If you say so…"

I nodded firmly.

April was quiet for a few moments, shifting the smaller plates of pickled vegetables in front of her. Content that we were finally on the same page, I returned to eating. April waited for me to start chewing, then said, "So what are you going to say when you see him again?"

I shrugged and continued focusing my attention on the juicy flavors in my mouth.

April waited patiently, unsatisfied with my shrug as an answer.

"Easy," I said. "I'm not going to see him again."

"You guys were like ten years old, he can't possibly still hold that against you. It's one thing if you were high school sweethearts who agreed to run away together, but you guys weren't even teenagers yet. We all do dumb things at that age. So what?"

"Making that promise was the last time I saw him," I pointed out, "and clearly I never showed."

"The two of you were so young, it's easy to hand-wave it away," she waved her chopsticks dismissively. "Just water under the bridge. Okay, okay, so it's a teeny bit awkward because some circumstances got in the way. There are worse things that could've happened, and..."

Some circumstances. The rest of April's comment was lost on me as I thought about how I hadn't exactly completely divulged all those circumstances to her. How the shakeup in Ethan's family was caused by *circumstances* that directly involved my family, specifically, my mother.

"Uh-huh," I managed to mumble, taking the opportunity to dig in on the pieces of meat that were ready for eating. Since I was shelling out for the meal, I intended to enjoy myself as much as I could, even if I didn't know what all the dishes were called.

April put her chopsticks down and crossed her arms in front of her chest as if I was the one being difficult. "Nev, you know I love you right?"

I pouted, knowing that whatever wisdom April was about to drop on me was probably something I wouldn't like.

"You can't just bury your head in the sand," she said. "He told you to wait for him. Those don't sound like the words of a man who doesn't want to see you again. And...wait..." April stopped to think to herself before shooting her attention back at me. "Was that sexual?"

I tilted my head at her.

April sucked in a small gasp. "It was totally sexual wasn't it?!" Her face lit up. "Oh my god, what if he wants you to *wait* before having sex with him? Like...he's teasing you, warming you up, getting you nice and ready for—"

"Shh!" I put my finger to my lips, my eyes scanning the neighboring tables for unwanted attention. "I don't think—"

April's eyes grew rounder as she continued, "And the ribbon! Oh, oh the ribbon! Maybe it's like a… like a cuff or… or a collar!"

If my ankles could blush, they would have.

Even though I took the stupid ribbon off when I got home, it still felt like it was there. The smooth feel of the silk resting on my ankle all the way from the hotel room to my apartment that night had done something to my sensitivities.

And it wasn't just my ankle.

Warmth filled my cheeks before spreading down to the parts of my body that remembered Ethan's touch that night. The way he grabbed me, forcefully on my arms, yet gently on my waist. How falling to the floor had felt strangely natural. Desperately wanting to strip his clothes off and equally wanting to be somehow punished for it.

I sure wanted to take my denim jacket off. The sudden heat up my back to the base of my neck was probably from sitting too close to the grill still searing meat in the middle of the table.

I crossed my arms again.

April made a growling noise that had no business coming from a human mouth, then grinned saucily at me, lowering her voice to the level of a dramatic whisper, "Maybe he wants to put his mark on you, claim you..."

The tightness I was feeling grew in the center of my chest. The squeeze against my ribs forced my breathing to become shallow as sweat beaded on my forehead. My jaw stiffened.

"Nobody can mark me," I spat the words out, louder than I'd expected. "I don't belong to anybody but myself." My eyes narrowed. "Nobody can mark me," I repeated. "Like I'm some kind of... some kind of... trinket in a rich guy's collection."

I hunched over the table and stared at the oil bubbling on the pork slices for a few deep breaths, forcing the tightness in my core to dissipate, before glancing back up to April.

"Sorry," I said.

What was I doing? I was making myself crazy for no reason at all. Ethan hadn't made it seem like he really wanted to control me, if anything, we had both just let things spiral out of control because of the silly game we were playing.

"Are you okay?" April asked, eyes wide and worried. She would've hugged me that instant if the table hadn't been in the way. "It could really just be a new beginning for you both, you know?" April offered with a supportive smile.

Maybe April was right. The past could just stay in the past. We were both grown adults now, practically strangers. I didn't need to be so defensive and worried about what hadn't even happened yet.

I sighed heavily. "You're probably right. You're always right."

"Aw…don't be like that Nev."

"No, it's true. It was stupid of me to assume that he wouldn't remember me and now I'm just avoiding owning up to that mistake, hoping that I won't see him again."

"There was definitely chemistry," April added.

"April."

"You know it and I know it too."

"Ugh, seriously, that was…"

"Just the heat of the moment! I get it. But it doesn't mean you have to shut down all opportunity. You can just take it slow and see where things go, if they go anywhere, you know?" She gave me a wide grin while serving me the cooked slices from the grill.

"Yeah, I know." I sighed and picked up one of the pieces from my plate. "What's this one?"

"Beef tongue."

I peeled my eyes wide at her. *"Tongue?"* I did a double take between the smoking piece of cooked tongue and April. "Wait…" I studied the little morsel. "Do I like this one? Or do I not like this one?"

"You definitely like that one." April giggled. "Don't worry, I know all the kinds of meat you like."

She prepared to wink at me just as the server stopped at our table and ended up delivering the wink straight to the older Korean woman.

"I'll get a fresh grill plate for your table," the woman said curtly before turning to the neighboring table.

"Yeesh, talk about awkward," April mumbled while I laughed. "See? Those awkward moments just fly away," she sang.

I nodded. "I'm not going to let it bother me. I just need to take things one step at a time."

"That's my girl!" April turned to grab the server's attention. "No need for a new grill plate, we'll just take the check please!"

Lingering Dreams

April once claimed that there were two kinds of people in the world: those who showered in the morning and those who showered at night.

According to her, it said a lot about your personality. People who showered in the morning were control freaks who wanted to make sure that they faced the world at their very best, while those who showered at night were more spontaneous, needing to refresh themselves after a day of adventures.

April usually showered at night, while I happened to shower in the morning. Though it seemed more like happenstance to me, it only confirmed her grand unifying theory about the nature of showers and personality type. My points about showering after working out, or showering at random times of day, or taking stress-relieving bubble baths had fallen on deaf ears.

I wondered what she'd say if she saw me now, taking evening showers in addition to my typical morning showers. Did it mean that I was a reformed control freak?

Unlikely.

Hot steam filled the air in front of my face while the pitter-patter of the shower rained around me. As I enjoyed the hot steam opening my sinuses, I couldn't help but think about the old days living with April and our shenanigans.

After college, April and I had spent years moving from rundown apartment to rundown apartment. If it wasn't the toilets suddenly seeping water from the bottom of the fixture, it was the air conditioning unit that needed a good smack. In the boiling L.A. summers, no one wanted to perform kickboxing moves just to get some cool air.

Then there was that one place we lived where someone had gotten shot a block away.

We broke the lease on that one.

April was usually content with the places I preferred, but since she started getting more acting gigs, she decided to move in with Roger and Philippe since they were willing to give her a good deal renting a room in their place in Burbank. She was closer to all the studios now, and I was proud of her even though I missed talking and laughing with her regularly without needing to plan a date outside of the shop.

When I stepped out of the shower, my skin prickled with goosebumps at the shock of the cold air and I wrapped myself up in my robe as quickly as I could. April had been busy this week with auditions, so we hadn't had a chance to chat beyond a few rushed conversations as we swapped shifts at the shop.

But luckily, work had prevented me from ruminating about Ethan and when I might see him again. It'd been a few days since our Korean BBQ night and though it had been easy to accept April's wisdom at the time, as the days passed, I had fallen back into old habits. I caught myself daydreaming during the day of disaster scenarios involving Ethan confronting me in embarrassing settings like the grocery checkout line and demanding that I answer for my broken promise as the checkout girl eyed us warily.

And facing bedtime had become a challenge, even though I'd felt exhausted from the day's work. Perhaps it was actually fatigue that made it harder to will myself to block out the inappropriate fantasies.

In the silence of my bedroom, thanks to my initiative last year to get better sleep, there were no distractions. Nothing to stop memories of Ethan rushing back. The boy I knew, and the man I just met again after so many years.

I sighed heavily and laid back on my bed.

At least some of the blame had to land on my dry spell recently. I'd hardly gone on any dates for the past six months, so was it any wonder that the one man I'd had a wrestling match with on the floor of his hotel room was now wrestling through my imagination night after night?

Usually I took care of myself when the need arose, but the encounter at the Imperial Grand had disoriented me far too much to take care of my basic needs.

It wasn't that I hadn't felt the mood strike. In fact, the dreams that kept me up at night were sexual to begin with. Grasping hands, sweat slick skin, the sharp tangy scent of musk. I'd wake up in the dark of night, my sheets soaked, my sex aching with heat. But every time I closed my eyes, reached my fingers down to take care of my need, Ethan's face would float into my vision.

Wait.

And then suddenly, I wouldn't want to touch myself anymore.

Maybe he wants to put his mark on you, claim you. April's words rang in my head.

In the safety of my bedroom, a shiver ran up my spine and I turtled deeper into my robe, suddenly conscious of my nakedness underneath.

No, Ethan Thorne didn't have some kind of sexual hold over me. That was absurd. It was just that I didn't want to give him the satisfaction of masturbating to fantasies of him, that's all. The only problem was that trying not to have any sexual thoughts only made my thoughts turn even more sexual. It was simple really.

And for a simple problem, I'd need a simple solution.

An orgasm.

Not just any orgasm, but I needed a mind blowing, eardrum shattering, toe curling orgasm.

Determined, I reached into my nightstand for Thumper, my favorite vibrator.

My hand fell upon a smooth soft surface, and my fingers brushed Thumper's silicone ears as I cradled the weight of my vibrator. When I brought out my familiar pink friend and held it in front of me, I realized that the silk ribbon that Ethan had tied around my ankle had been lying on top Thumper all this time.

The crimson slip of fabric peaked out of my fingers and dangled innocently down the back of my hand, tickling my wrist.

My head whirled with emotions from that night. After returning from the Imperial Grand, I had torn the ribbon off and stuffed it in the nightstand. It hadn't crossed my mind that I might see it in there at some point, but it was certainly inappropriate timing.

I separated Thumper from the ribbon, resting him comfortably in my lap, then held the red strip between two fingers and watched it sway in front of my face. The crimson shine of fabric looked foreign in my bedroom. The silk ribbon had started off on a simple spool in my shop and rightfully belonged to me. Yet even so, Ethan had plucked it from the floor, carried it close the entire night, and then tied it onto my skin.

It belonged to him.

I'd brought a piece of Ethan back into my home.

I tossed the ribbon on top of my nightstand and stared defiantly at it.

Could April have been right? Was Ethan trying to claim me by tying the ribbon around my ankle? Did he want to take me? Own me? Claim me? The questions multiplied, swirling through my head but the question that scared me the most was: What would it feel like to give in to Ethan, to surrender to him?

And would I — would I enjoy it?

Ethan's eyes, boring into me, watching me as I spread my legs. Heavy breathing as I offered myself to him, his lips moving, saying something...

Cum for me.

My hand brushed against Thumper's switch and my eyes shot open. I threw my vibrator across the room, and it rumbled on the floor. My cheeks were flushed with heat as if Ethan were really there, staring at me.

No way I was going to give him the satisfaction of getting me this worked up over a stupid ribbon. No way in hell was I under Ethan Thorne's thumb. Besides, I had no idea what the ribbon had been about anyway, it was in the heat of the moment and just because April thought it was something sexual didn't mean anything.

In fact, I hardly knew anything about Ethan Thorne, despite what had happened at the Conservation Fund event. We were strangers now, just two people who had an awkward encounter, that's all.

The Climb

The next morning I found myself in a Chinatown back alley, jiggling the doorknob to a solid steel door. I was used to getting up at an eye-crusty early hour to take flower deliveries at the shop, but being wide awake while the sky was still grey and dark was a rarity. After a night of tossing and turning, I expected to be groggy and tired this morning, but instead, my body felt abnormally jittery.

It wasn't difficult to figure out what I was anxious about, or rather *who*.

Which was how I ended up in the alley behind Rise, the local rock climbing gym where I was a regular. I'd been climbing since college, which was why April had taken to calling me "Nev," after the Sierra Nevada mountain range. Though I usually preferred the thrill and challenge of climbing outdoors, I couldn't deny the convenience of getting my workouts done on indoor walls. It'd been more than a couple of weeks since I'd had a good sweat, which probably contributed to my antsiness.

Maybe all I needed to stop having these sexual fantasies about Ethan was a round of intense cardio. At the very least, it'd help me work off the extra calories from Korean BBQ.

I unlocked the back door to Rise and clicked on half the lights. Even though I was a key-holding member, and was entitled to come and go as I pleased, I still felt guilty for using up too much electricity when I was going to be the only one at the gym.

Since there wasn't anyone available to belay for me on the main wall, so I settled for the bouldering walls, which were low enough to climb without a safety harness. I set my small backpack down on the mat, chalked up my hands and picked a random route.

Before I realized it, I'd finished the climb and found myself wondering what Ethan's typical workout routine was. Shaking aside the thought, I started on a more difficult route, but as I hung off the faux rock handles on the wall, I had a flash of an absurd image of crimping my fingers into Ethan's abs in order to climb his torso like a rock wall.

Desperate to escape my thoughts, I picked another route at random and started climbing immediately.

"Sweet lines, Spider-woman!" A loud voice echoed through the open space.

All of the lights in the entire gym flicked on one by one as I jumped off onto the mat. I turned around to see Russell Pembleton loping over with smooth long strides, a big goofy grin on his face.

He was wearing a horizontal striped tank top, board shorts, and flip-flops, like he'd just strolled off the beach and onto the Santa Monica boardwalk. Before I met him, I didn't think it was possible for someone to be as laid-back as Russell.

Russell usually worked at the front desk when he wasn't studying for his Master's degree in sports medicine. Apparently he'd spent most of his twenties chasing waves and climbing the best spots across the country, before he decided to choose a more practical career. That didn't mean that he'd given up on his favorite activities though.

I hadn't been expecting company, but then again, in my current state of mind, the distraction was welcome.

Maybe some of Russell's laid-back attitude would even rub off on me.

"Hey Russell," I said. "I didn't think you'd be here so early."

"My shift doesn't start for a bit, but I wanted to find somewhere quiet to study. The roomies are recreating Woodstock '69 on the living room couch."

If I were being honest, I had no idea what it was like to walk in on roommates bumping uglies since April and I had been very respectful roomies for as long as I could remember.

I chuckled politely. "I know how that goes."

He presented me a friendly fist, which I bumped.

"Hey, need a belayer?" he asked.

"Oh no, it's alright," I said, "I figured I'd just tinker around on the bouldering wall."

"Patrick says it's part of my job description to chat up the regulars and belay for them," Russell said, winking at me, "says it's good for business. And you know Patrick, he hates merely content customers more than unhappy ones."

"Sounds like Patrick," I agreed. Patrick O'Neill, the white haired owner of the gym, had been climbing since his teens and I always admired how he ran a tight ship.

"So how 'bout it?"

Russell's offer was pretty tempting. To be honest, I'd worked the routes on the bouldering wall so many times over that I could practically do them in my sleep. They were hardly challenging enough to keep my mind off of Ethan. If I could harness in and climb the main wall… Maybe then I could even experience a few moments of zen.

"You sure?" I asked, still a bit reluctant. It was certainly nice of Russell to offer to belay, but I didn't want to get in the way of his plans. "Didn't you need to study?"

Russell shook his head, his blond curls swishing back and forth. "Nah, it's probably overkill at this point. I just gotta go with the flow and trust that I've studied enough. Mostly I just wanted to get out of the house. C'mon you gotta have a project in the Pit."

"You've sold me," I said, laughing. "Thanks, Russell."

Russell pumped his fist and we made our way to the Pit. "The Pit" was an area that had stairs down to the lower level and a much higher wall. There was a top rope bolted to the ceiling, which allowed one person to stay on the ground to belay for the harnessed climber, who could climb nearly three stories into the air without fear of injury.

Once I got to the bottom of my route on the main wall, I strapped my harness in and Russell did likewise, hooking himself to the brake and other end of the top rope.

Russell waited patiently and quietly, while I studied the route, visualizing my ascent. The main difficulty I had with this route was a tricky section near the end of the climb, I didn't know if it was the fact that it was so high or just the technical challenge, but I hadn't been able to master it yet. Maybe it had something to do with having to commit myself to a jump so high up in the air. Even though I knew Russell was a highly experienced climber, and by definition an excellent belayer, looking at the final stretch of the climb still gave me the heebie jeebies.

Seemed like exactly the kind of challenge I needed to set my mind straight.

I gave Russell the thumbs up, chalked up my hands and started up the wall.

Before long, each hold gave way to another hold, and I entered into the comfortable groove of pushing my skills to the limit. Soon, I began to feel the familiar burn in my muscles as the wall filled my entire vision.

Up here, working to the edge of my comfort zone was almost like a kind of meditation.

It reminded me of why I'd started climbing in the first place. When I'm climbing at the edge of my abilities, there's no space for me to carry all of the baggage from my outside life up with me. No worries about upcoming gigs, no worries about embarrassing myself, no worries about my lackluster love life.

Certainly no room to picture Ethan's dark, piercing gaze, under those shapely brows, or the curve of his sensuous mouth as it twisted with humor as if he was telling himself some joke only he could understand. Or wonder how he'd known exactly who I was the entire night we'd spent at the charity event. Or speculate on why he'd keep it a secret from me the whole night.

I slipped.

There was only the sensation of open space for a moment before the rope snapped taut and the harness dug into my butt.

I spun in the air for a few rotations, then swung myself back to the wall and rappelled down.

Once on the ground, I aimed a frustrated kick at the wall. Apparently, cardio wasn't the answer to all my problems.

I craned my neck up to see the spot where I'd screwed up. It'd been barely a quarter of the way up the route, a section that I thought I'd mastered already. It'd been a while since I'd been at the wall but at least I expected to get past the halfway mark.

"Tough break," Russell said, making sympathetic sounds. "First climb in a while, huh?"

I nodded, a little breathless, wondering if it was that obvious that I was out of shape.

Russell studied the route quietly for a few seconds. "Don't worry, Sierra, you'll get it. Sometimes it just takes a while to get back into the swing of things."

"Any tips for getting there faster?"

Russell shrugged. "Just gotta go with the flow."

Upstream

The bell jingled musically when I pushed the door open at Venus Floral Design. I was greeted with the subtle sweet smell of tulips underneath the grassy scent of freshly cut stems. The flower shop always made me feel at home, no matter how my day was going.

April was bent over the computer behind the counter, with only the top of her head visible, her hair wrapped in a neat bun.

"Just a second, ma'am, I'll be with you shortly," she called over the counter without looking up. I could hear her clacking on the keyboard.

I plopped my purse on the counter and announced in a snooty voice, "Ugh, sure, it's not like you have a paying customer or anything!"

April popped up from her seat, wide-eyed.

She relaxed visibly when she registered that it was me. "Jeeze, Nev, you scared me half to death. I thought you were the lizard lady returned," she said, watching me carefully.

I hung my purse on a hook underneath the counter. When I stood up, April was studying me so intently that I felt a bit uncomfortable.

"Did something happen? Any trouble makers?" I asked, concerned.

"No, no, everything was wonderful. Oh, I mean, it was pretty chill. Just a couple of walk-ins. Sold a few of the extra bouquets that we prepped for the charity event and we got that delivery of red roses earlier than expected. I've already stripped most of them so..."

I noticed April hesitate, studying the area, and then move the box of unstripped roses before sitting in the seat that would face me.

"You're doing that thing," I said.

"What thing?"

"The studying-each-of-my-movements thing."

April casually tucked some loose hair strands behind her ear. "It just seems like you're in a great mood, that's all. How was your workout?"

"It was tough getting back into it," I said, letting my eyes wander to the flowers by the front window, "but I'm going with the flow. Thanks for taking the earlier shift."

April seemed to accept my answer—despite the fact that I didn't remember the last time I said the words "go with the flow"—and nodded. "Good! I'm glad you're feeling better. I'm going to take some credit for that." She hummed a few perky notes.

I smiled in return before asking, "Aren't you going to be late for your audition?"

April pouted. "You don't want me hanging around anymore?"

"Well, of course I'd rather you hang out, but if you miss your audition, how am I ever going to see you on the silver screen? How am I going to see your name in lights? How am I going to help you pick out your red carpet dress?"

She grinned and started gathering her stuff. "Oh, I almost forgot. Someone booked a consultation after regular hours tonight at five or five-thirty. It's in the appointment book."

"Got it, thanks for the heads up."

"And don't forget," April sang from the front door. "Kronuts tomorrow morning!"

After April left, I responded to a few inquiries I wanted to handle personally and checked the appointment calendar to confirm a five-thirty appointment with a Mr. Stephen Reinsmar. I placed a few binders of sample bouquets on the counter, making sure they included both specific event suggestions and arrangements organized by dominant color.

I put on some smooth jazz and then started stripping the rest of the roses, humming to myself as I worked. Thanks to April, the roses took hardly any time at all. I ended up spending longer breaking down the cardboard boxes and tying them up with the rest of our recycling.

April had gone out of her way to take care of other loose ends around the shop, really freeing up my time. I walked around the shop checking the flowers on display and allowing myself to be a bit detail oriented about each vase. It was one of my favorite low-stress tasks. When I was finished, I ritualistically stood in the center of my shop, hands on my hips, and took it all in.

A feeling of pride never failed to fill my chest at what I had built.

What *April* and I had built together.

At five o'clock, I went to the front, flipped the sign from "OPEN" to "CLOSED" in preparation for the consultation, and then pulled the door open to collect our foldable chalkboard sign.

Walking toward the front door, was Ethan Thorne.

Alter-egos

Ethan wore a casual pair of khaki slacks, a brown belt, and a light blue shirt. Even though he was no longer outfitted in the same formal wear as that night at the charity ball, he was still a sight to behold. His hair was loosely tousled, not messy, yet not formally styled, contrasting with his clean shaven jaw line.

He stopped at the door. I caught a whiff of his cologne with a passing breeze. The scent instantly transported me to that hazy night more than a week ago in the Imperial Grand Hotel when—for a brief moment—we'd been skin against skin, breath against breath, lips against lips.

But now the haze had lifted and everything was illuminated in the light of day.

And on the sunny 5600 block of El Camino in Los Angeles we watched each other awkwardly, him outside my shop, me safely inside, the door ajar between us.

For a beat neither of us knew what to say, but he flashed me a relaxed smile. I suddenly remembered the feeling of his calloused hands, heavy against my ribcage.

Blood rushed to my cheeks and I fought the instinct to pretend like I hadn't seen him.

Fat chance of selling that one.

"Hi," said Ethan.

"I'm sorry, um. We're closed. I mean," I shook my head, "I'm still going to be here, but we're by appointment only after five so... I guess we're not *technically* closed but uh... are you... what are you here for?"

Smooth Sierra, real smooth.

Ethan leaned over in order to avoid talking to me from behind the door and presented his cellphone. There was an email open. I could feel him watching me as I scanned the screen.

The email was a standard confirmation for appointments. Specifically, an appointment at our shop: Venus Floral Design.

My consultation for the evening was *Ethan Thorne*?

But that was ridiculous, I'd checked the appointment book and the name was definitely Stephen Reinsmar. I always made a point of learning my client names before their meetings.

"There must be some sort of mistake," I said scanning the email again. Sure enough, the reservation was for Stephen Reinsmar. "Yes, this confirmation is for someone else."

Ethan cracked a grin at me through the door. "Alter-egos have their uses, especially for someone in my position." He helpfully added, "I'm sure you understand."

Was that a jab at me?

Calling April's nickname for me an "alter-ego" would have been stretching it, but I could see where he might get that idea from.

I reminded myself not to jump to conclusions in my panicked state.

It wasn't that uncommon for celebrities to use pseudonyms to make reservations in order to avoid the paparazzi or crazed fans. Even our little shop had gotten a few of those. Booking an appointment under a different name could have been entirely innocent — Ethan Thorne's standard operating procedure. Either way I had to wrestle with the fact the he'd decided to show up right here at my shop. Of course, I'd expected to hear from Ethan again after how our last meeting had ended, but I still wasn't ready. I thought I'd have more time.

And wasn't Ethan the type of guy who was very busy?

Which begged the question: Why was he here? To talk? Talk about what?

"May I come in?" Ethan asked. "It's a little hot out here."

I realized that I was leaning my entire weight against the barely open door, as if bracing myself against it might be a good defense against having Ethan in my flower shop. At the same moment, I realized that *he* must've been pushing equally hard to keep the door open. Embarrassed, I relented. Ethan, consciously or unconsciously, eased off as well.

"Yes, of course, come in," I said, stepping back and swinging the door open, my mind racing through the possible reasons that Ethan could have wanted to make an appointment. I'd promised April that I'd keep an open mind, and I had resolved to go with the flow, but I wasn't exactly prepared for whatever this was.

And what if he was here to confront me about the past?

Sorry about that minor incident fifteen years ago when I told you we'd run away together but I ditched you instead... Kids do the darndest thing, am I right? P.S. You're a great kisser.

Or what if he was here to talk about the more recent past, when we'd almost had sex in his hotel room?

I couldn't decide which would be worse.

The bells on the door frame tinkled softly as Ethan stepped into the shop.

He blinked a few times to adjust to the dimmer lighting. Then his eyes made a slow, meticulous sweep over the interior.

From the side, I couldn't see his face clearly, but I imagined the same dark, intense expression that had demanded a response from my body. Though his gaze wasn't directed at me, I felt naked and vulnerable, as if by allowing Ethan in, I was baring an intimate part of myself to him.

The shop that I'd been so proud of immediately felt shabby. The storefront looked crowded and disorganized rather than small and cozy as I'd intended. The display tables were dusty, excess water had pooled around a few vases, and the floor was still peppered with residual leaves from the roses I'd just stripped.

I regretted that I'd put off the final sweep until after the consultation.

I wanted to explain myself, to tell him that most of our business was from events, and that the storefront was just a place for us to meet with potential clients, that it was more of a workshop than anything else.

"I see," he murmured to himself, as he surveyed the interior, walking deeper into the shop. I hurried after him, trying to collect my thoughts.

Ethan stopped in front of the bucket of roses I'd prepared earlier. I stopped behind him, wringing my hands nervously. He selected a single rose, plucking it up by the stem, cradling it delicately in both hands as if it would shatter if he were to drop it.

He tilted his head at me. "Don't these come with thorns?"

"Yes, we always strip the thorns."

"Why?"

"For easier handling and enjoyment by clients," I said. "People usually enjoy the blooms themselves, and prefer not to deal with the thorns, because they—"

"Might get pricked?" Ethan fingered a stub of a cut thorn on the stem of the rose.

I couldn't tell if he was making a joke about his own name or not, like: Ethan Thorne, the consummate prick. So I just nodded slowly.

Ethan turned to me.

"Tell me, how do people like to enjoy the bloom?"

"Um…just by its appearance mostly, but you can also smell it, and…"

Touch it.

Feel the petals between your fingers.

I kept my mouth shut as Ethan held the flower up to his nose. It brought to mind images of him sampling the glass of expensive scotch at the hotel bar when he'd had a similar expression on his face. After a moment, Ethan opened his eyes and examined the petals carefully, his eyes so focused he was probably making the rose nervous.

Ethan brushed his fingers against the outer petals, taking his time, feeling, almost massaging, the velvety texture.

I almost broke a sweat trying hard not to let my imagination run wild. I wanted to say something, but he seemed so intensely focused, I wasn't sure if I should interrupt.

Finally, he turned to face me, running his index finger slowly down the smooth stem.

"It's my first time inside a flower shop," he said, a hint of humor at the crook of his mouth, as if he were sharing a private joke with me.

I raised a skeptical eyebrow at him.

"It's the truth," he said. "One of my assistants usually handles these kind of things."

Now that he'd turned to face me, I was reminded of how he'd made me feel, how easy it was to fall into his dark eyes.

Was I getting pulled in by some inescapable force, or were we just standing a little too close for a flower shop owner and potential client?

I smiled politely and backed away from him, conscious of all the premade arrangements around me in vases. No sense in having a repeat of the other night.

There would be no accidents or games this time.

"I see. Well, welcome to my shop. I assume you got my information from Giselle?" I started, uncomfortable with the ball being in my court. "I have to say, I'm surprised to see you. I, uh..." I stumbled over my words trying to figure out how to ask him why he had shown up without sounding too antagonistic.

Ethan's face shifted, then he placed the rose he had been inspecting back with the others.

"Work has me stuck in town until a certain deal is resolved, and I found myself in need of flowers." He grinned at me. "And seeing as you are the best florist I know in Los Angeles..."

Jeez, cool it Nev, he's just here as a regular customer.

Here I was, imagining the worst case scenario, when Ethan just wanted some flowers. This consultation would be like any other. I could get into the zone and take care of business as usual. There'd be no confrontations, no games, no intense sexual tension. I was just making it all up in my head.

We would be two normal adults handling some everyday business.

I let my shoulders down and gave Ethan my usual charming smile for clients. "Well, thank you for selecting our shop for you needs! This must be for someone very special for you to come yourself."

"Sometimes you need to go out of your way to keep the best people."

"Oh, will this be for an employee of yours?"

"Yes, for Nicole. You remember?"

Ah yes, the assistant we were trying to avoid that night at the Conservation Fund. That night we ran away like a couple of kids avoiding our parents. That night we got a bit too carried away in your hotel room. *That night.*

Ethan continued, "I'm not...the easiest person to work for, and she's had a difficult time recently. I figured she'd appreciate it."

"She must be a great employee," I said stiffly. "Will this be a loose bouquet or will you also require a vase?" I was usually smoother with my idle chit chat, but I was rattled by having Ethan in my shop.

Ethan sat down at one of the tall stools next to the counter. "I'd like a vase. That one specifically."

He pointed to a classic-shaped glass vase with a flared out opening. The same style that I'd broken that night. It had to be a coincidence. There was no way that he remembered the shape of the vase from the Conservation Fund event. I reminded myself not to jump to conclusions. It was possible that Ethan was deliberately messing with me, but more likely, he just enjoyed the way the vase looked.

"And do you have any specific flowers in mind?" I asked.

He stared at me, silent.

It had to have been a few seconds, but I could feel my skin getting hot and that uncomfortable itch in my legs to impulsively shake my limbs out like I was at the climbing wall.

"If not, I can make some suggestions," I added quickly. He did say it was his first time in a flower shop after all. "If you're commending your employee on a job well done," I continued, "I'd recommend bright sunshine colors like yellow and orange to send the appropriate message."

"The appropriate message," Ethan repeated my words in a soft murmur between contemplation and musing.

I decided to interpret the lack of criticism as agreement and continued with my standard script. I gestured to the small display on the counter. "We provide cards that you can include with the arrangement if you'd like to write something for the recipient while I prepare the bouquet."

I turned around to start working on the arrangement and didn't hear any form of protest from Ethan. I picked the flowers leisurely, buying myself time to think, but mostly to get my pulse under control. Forcing myself to hum while I worked, I reminded myself that everything was just fine.

After I finished preparing the arrangement, I was about to select a ribbon to tie around the neck of the vase, when I thought it better to leave it as it was.

I set the arrangement on the higher counter and presented it to Ethan.

He nodded, silently inspecting the flowers, seemingly happy with how it came out.

"I hope it's to your liking," I said, tapping the cost of the flowers into a calculator. "That'll be…"

Ethan slid his credit card over to me before I could finish. "Whatever the cost, it's worth it."

"I'm glad you're satisfied," I said, maintaining my professional poise, charged the card, and handed it back to him. This everyday exchange that I was so used to day-in-and-day-out afforded me the space to gather my thoughts.

Ethan might have come to get flowers for his assistant, but I had a feeling that there was an ulterior motive behind it as well.

Ethan and I had both changed. We weren't children anymore, so we could handle whatever this new relationship was like adults. We did let things get a little out of hand, resulting in this awkward situation, but we could put all our cards on the table and have a frank discussion. And if I broached the topic first, at least I'd have some control over the direction.

"Listen, Ethan," I said, "I don't know when we'll see each other again so I just wanted to clear the air."

"Where's the ribbon?" he asked, his eyes still on the flowers.

"O-Oh," I stumbled, "you wanted a ribbon on the vase." I swiftly grabbed a precut ribbon and tied it onto the vase before he could respond.

Ethan set the flowers aside.

Then he lifted his face to mine, his eyes pinning me to the spot. "And the other ribbon? Have you been wearing it?"

I could almost feel the soft slip of fabric around my ankle, as if Ethan was gripping my bare skin. A flood of heat rushed to my sex at the thought of being claimed by him. My face flushed. My body felt hot, reliving that heat that ripped through my body when Ethan had pinned my body to the floor, feeling his need rub against me, sensing my desire.

I closed my eyes, took a breath and then opened my eyes to look at him again. His face was familiar, yet uncannily different and strange. This Ethan Thorne was nothing like the sweet boy I knew as a child. I'd wondered for many nights who Ethan Thorne had become. And now I knew. Perhaps I'd always known but had just been afraid to admit it to myself.

Though I'd wanted to clear the air with Ethan and talk about that evening, it was clear to me now that we had very different ideas about the meaning of what had transpired.

"Ethan, that…that was a mistake," I said, finally.

He was quiet for a moment, his eyes intense, like he could read my thoughts.

I shook my head. "I'm sorry, I should have been more straightforward with you about—" My mouth suddenly felt dry and I forced myself to swallow. "We should have never played those games. I should have…"

Though we'd both gotten lost in games that night, we were playing for very different stakes. I couldn't treat him like he was the same naive boy, and I was no longer the same naive girl. There was far more at risk. Perhaps these were the types of games that this grown up version of Ethan enjoyed playing. Games of risk and reward, cat and mouse, danger and sex.

But they were far too much for me.

Ethan did not relent, coming closer until I could feel my skin prickling from our bodies so close together. "I can sense your need, your arousal. If that night was a mistake, then why did you wait for me? I can end your need, I can show you things, make the wait worth your while..."

His voice seemed to resonate in my chest, making my vision swim, overwhelming me with a sense of vertigo.

Quietly, I said, "You don't know me," and pushed the vase back across the counter. "Please take your flowers and leave, Mr. Thorne."

My instinct that night had been to say goodbye and tie up loose ends.

It was the right choice.

He was different.

I was different.

There was no possibility of reconciling who we'd become.

"If that's what you want." Ethan took the vase, turned and walked to the door, stopping just before he left, hesitating just inside the threshold. "We spend so much of our lives showing a mask to the world, perhaps it is only in our mistakes that our truest selves are revealed."

First, Donuts

"Don't worry Nev! Once we get these fluffy donuts into our bellies, you'll feel so much better," April said, patting her tummy and rubbing it dramatically. Out of the corner of my eye, I saw her reaching over to rub my stomach.

"I'm trying to drive here," I grumbled.

Her hand froze and she slumped back into the passenger seat.

"Sorry, I just need my morning coffee," I said, feeling slightly guilty that I wasn't playing along with April's silliness like I usually did.

I'd spent most of the drive over talking April's ear off about Ethan's impromptu visit until I was sick of my own voice. For some reason, instead of feeling better for getting it off my chest, I was only getting crankier with each passing minute.

That probably had something to do with the fact that I'd spent most of the night tossing and turning, imagining the things I *could* have said to Ethan, instead of sleeping. Naturally, I'd overslept, forcing me to skip my sacred ritual of brewing my own coffee.

With everything that had happened, a hot, fragrant cup of coffee was a necessity, not a luxury. This legendary donut shop that April was so excited about had better serve some decent Joe.

It was only after I parked and we made our way to the shop that we saw the line.

Every single hipster that lived within a twenty-mile radius had decided to congregate on this one donut shop in order to prevent me from getting my coffee. The line seemed to stretch on farther than the eye could see, like we were all waiting to take a selfie with a Kardashian.

April patted me consolingly on my back. "This just means the donuts will be all the sweeter," she said, ever the optimist.

I let out a loud groan as we took our spots at the end of the line, trying not to think about how much longer it would take before I could get that cup.

April looked at me cautiously. "You believe me about yesterday right? He really didn't sound the same at all on the phone, honest."

"No, I drove across town, picked you up before seven in the morning, and delayed my morning coffee because I just know you were in on it with Ethan."

"I don't know... Gourmet donuts can be pretty compelling..."

I raised an eyebrow at her.

"Okay, okay, you're right, *I'm* the donut monster. Om nom nom!" April wrapped her arms around me and gave me a big hug. "Thank you for driving us all the way here. I wish you would have texted me last night! We really could have come here some other day."

"It's alright," I said, letting April's hug comfort me, though she was squeezing my rib cage a bit too hard. "I know you've been looking forward to this all week. I'll have coffee in me soon enough and god knows I could use a distraction anyway."

April let go of me and put both hands on my shoulders, her face serious, her eyes concerned. "Listen to me, Nev, you did the right thing with Ethan."

I craned my neck, tip toeing to see over April's head, counting the number of people in line ahead of us so I wouldn't have to think about what she was saying.

"Uh huh," I mumbled. I did some quick estimates. Assuming that the cashier took three minutes with every guest...then we'd be at the front of the line by...

April furrowed her eyebrows at me. "It wasn't your fault," she said, pausing and waiting for me to respond.

The line would be more efficient if they had two cashiers and moved one of those extra employees floating around the back to the coffee station. It seemed that there was a large hold up at the coffee station where customers used unpracticed hands to pour themselves coffee and fumble with caps and cream and sugar packets. Then, after making it past that station without spilling coffee or cream all over the place, anyone who got to the front of the line would hem and haw over the donut flavors, holding up everyone behind them.

I resisted the urge to run up to the front and rearrange everybody myself. But if I were running this event, I'd be juggling the attendees' happiness with the appearance of popularity with the line wrapped around the corner. I did a slow sweep of the area and figured I'd probably have large signs or banners in addition to balloons.

Did any thought go into this at all?

The obvious lack of foresight was all so aggravating, so intensely frustrating, so...stupid! Pressure felt like it was building in me like my chest was a whistling kettle, with the spout screaming in a crescendo, ready to explode

"What did I expect really?" I said sharply, surprising even myself. The man wearing a green plaid shirt in front of us turned around, eyeing me warily.

"The guy regularly attends soirees with ticket prices that cost more than I make a year, and he drinks fancy whiskies that were bottled before I was even born! How could it have worked out anyway? Who needs that kind of stress! Sure, we had some harmless fun together as kids, but that doesn't mean that he's the same person I knew or that he knows anything about me! How dare he—" I wrung my arms in the air angrily.

I released a guttural sigh and looked at April sadly, who saddled up next to me and gently rubbed my back.

"Oh, Nev. Do you feel better now?"

"I dunno," I said, my shoulders slumped. "I guess so."

April made a sympathetic sound while nodding in agreement. "Hey, look," she said, motioning with her chin, "the line is actually moving fairly quickly, we're almost at the coffee station."

She was right. This wasn't opening day for the shop and they probably knew how to handle the line. I was just getting all out of sorts, but I felt a bit better after that release. And now, I could just finally seal it off with some coffee.

At the coffee station, there was only the shop's "house coffee" being offered which made the decision making process nonexistent. I slid two coffee cups off the stack and handed one to April before filling up my own cup. Needing my coffee fix, I immediately took my habitual sip and almost gagged. I snapped the cap on top.

Obviously this place wasn't known for its coffee.

The unexpected revulsion froze up my body and April had to forcefully nudge me so she could access the overflowing basket of cream and sugars.

"You're going to need a lot of those," I said bitterly. "No wonder the basket is so large, this is awful."

"Oh no, really?" She dug frantically into the creamer basket.

"Yeah, wow, this is really..." I let my eyes wander around the shop. The loud pastel colors in addition to the wood tables and exposed rafter beams and bare light bulbs hanging from the ceiling just *screamed* hipster. It just screamed that they had the best coffee around. I didn't even consider that the coffee could be *this* bad. I was so convinced that this was going to make everything better.

"This is really...disappointing," I said softly.

"I'm so sorry, Nev!" April burst in. "When we get to the shop I'll—"

"No," I firmly cut her off. "It's not the coffee."

April recapped her coffee after filling it to the brim with creamer and looked at me questioningly. "You're disappointed about Ethan."

I sighed deeply and let the feeling sit in. "I stupidly held onto some fantasy that somehow we could work it out. I was expecting some kind of fantasy, and maybe Ethan was expecting a different kind of fantasy, too. So of course we'd both end up...disappointed."

"It's okay to feel that way, Nev," April said. "Just feel the feeling, accept it, and let it pass. Let it pass with donuts. Because these donuts are on me, baby!"

I let myself crack a smile as April whipped out her list and started making our order since we had finally made it to the cashier. Now it was our turn to hold up the line as April hemmed and hawed over our order. Even if the coffee was terrible, at the very least I knew the donuts were going to taste better.

Second, Coffee

April stuffed the final piece of her creme brulee donut into her mouth and tucked the entire donut box under her arm when we heard a knock at the back door.

I gave her a questioning look. Was she really going to keep eating donuts while we moved the flowers in?

"Anton might want some," she explained, her mouth still full.

Anton was the delivery man from our supplier and a huge film buff. Middle-aged and always cheerful, he and April would catch up on the latest releases whenever he dropped off our flowers. As far as I was concerned, anyone who could help us finish the nearly two dozen donuts April had ordered was a saint.

We walked out back to the alleyway to see a familiar white box truck straight ahead, parked along the opposite brick wall. A young man stood by the back wearing a white tank top and black track pants with a jacket tied around his waist. His muscular arms were covered with colorful tattoos.

That definitely wasn't Anton.

He quickly jogged over, across the narrow alley, to where we were standing. "You have delivery today, yes?" he asked with a light accent. Contrary to his casual look, the man's demeanor was all professional; his posture would have made a drill sergeant proud.

"That's right," I said, "What happened to Anton?"

"Sorry, I'm new," the man said. "I don't know so much. Perhaps family problem, I hear."

I shrugged at April, expecting her to be a bit disappointed. I knew she looked forward to shooting the shit with our usual delivery guy, but seeing her now, slack jawed, gawking at our new delivery man, I wondered if she still remembered who Anton was.

April had that very April look in her eye.

I elbowed her in the ribs, before she started drooling, and offered my hand to the new guy. "Well, I'm Sierra, as the invoice probably says. It's good to meet you…uh…"

"Nikolas," the young man said, pumping my hand up and down once, all business.

April finally shook the dazed look from her face and opened the donut box, presenting it to Nikolas rather than shaking his hand.

"Would you like some donuts?" she chirped. "We just went to the Krusty Kronut today and stood in line for a half hour so we could nab some Kronuts. If you like more traditional donuts, the red velvet flavor is delicious, but if you prefer chocolate, they said that the cookies and cream flavor is pretty spectacular too..."

Nikolas took a step back, looked at April cautiously, then back at the donuts. "Thank you, but that won't be necessary," he said stiffly. "Um...perhaps I can show you the delivery, I have invoice for you." He presented a clipboard to me which I looked over briefly.

"Don't worry about her," I said, motioning to April to put the donuts down. "She sometimes has a bit of an overwhelming effect on people."

I followed Nikolas to the back of the truck and raised an eyebrow at April. She bit her bottom lip and fanned herself dramatically. Secretly, I was glad to see her swooning over a guy for a change, especially after all the fuss about me and Ethan.

Things were finally getting back to their usual swing.

After Nikolas had rolled up the door to the back of the truck, he helpfully slid a loading-ramp down so that we wouldn't have to climb up. Once we had made our way up the ramp, the three of us stood in the back, while Nikolas showed me the boxes, diligently checking off each item against the yellow invoice with a ballpoint pen.

As I verified the list against the receipt in my email, April stood on the opposite side of Nikolas, doing a few too many once-overs.

"Looks good, everything's here," I said. "We'll help you unload and let you be on your way."

"N-Nice ink," April stuttered.

To a stranger it would have seemed like any old forgettable slip-up in conversation, but I knew that April hardly ever stuttered. She had a habit of getting shy when using her flirtatious voice with men she found attractive, especially when it wasn't written in a script.

Nikolas half-smiled uncomfortably and muttered a polite thank you.

Eager to give April and Nikolas some space before I got caught up in their swirling vortex of passion, I grabbed the top box, long and rectangular and filled with pink geraniums, and headed back to the shop, grinning to myself. I couldn't wait to poke fun at April later.

Turns out April had been right, the day had been getting better and better ever since we got those donuts.

As soon as I reached the bottom of the ramp, I saw him.

Ethan Thorne, standing at the back door of my shop, two coffees in hand, wearing a green and navy argyle sweater. He looked different, more relaxed than the other day, though his clothing was only marginally more casual.

I almost tripped but played it off as if I'd planned on hopping off the last section of the ramp.

Either Ethan was planning on drinking both of those coffees or one of them was for me. No way was I ready to face the prickliest billionaire on the west coast this early in the day. With the flower box under my arm, I marched toward my shop, heading across the alley as if I couldn't see him.

He didn't step out of the way, and for a moment, I considered bowling him over using the long cardboard box as a battering ram. But I figured the liability of cracking Ethan Thorne's skull on the asphalt was not worth the brief moment of satisfaction.

Ethan started, "Hi —"

I cleared my throat loudly, cutting him off.

He looked at me, slightly confused, still blocking the doorway.

Once more, without making eye contact, I cleared my throat, jabbing the box of geraniums toward him and gesturing with my chin toward the door.

"Ah, of course, I'm in your way," he said, stepping aside.

I breezed by him, without giving him a second glance like he was just some pesky fly.

Inside my shop, I set the geraniums down on the large steel work table, and turned on my heel to head back outside for another box. If I slowed down long enough to think, I'd lose my nerve and end up locking all the doors to the shop, barricading Ethan safely outside.

Clearly that wasn't an option because the rest of our flower delivery needed to be prepped and refrigerated, not to mention that would leave April locked outside as well. Then again, maybe she would appreciate some alone time with Nikolas.

I spent longer debating with myself than I was proud of, but reason won out in the end. What kind of friend would I be to lock April outside just so I wouldn't have to have an awkward encounter with Ethan?

I shot out of the back door, making a beeline for the truck, determined to focus only on unloading the truck. It would be quick and simple, like usual, I tried to convince myself.

Ethan was just a minor inconvenience.

"Sierra," Ethan said my name firmly, while standing immediately to block my way. "I just want to talk."

I tried to step around him, but it wasn't hard for Ethan to effortlessly block my way with his large frame.

I took a deep breath and aimed a piercing glare straight into Ethan's eyes. "We're busy here," I said between clenched teeth, hot blood pumping through my veins.

Ethan set the coffees he was holding gently on the ground, safely by the wall, like I might just grab them out of his hands and throw them at him.

"Look," he began, putting his hands out placatingly.

Then Nikolas stacked a box rather suddenly into Ethan's waiting arms.

I waved my hand at Nikolas. "Oh no, he doesn't work here."

"He...not assistant? Bring coffee for you and donut girl?" Nikolas asked.

"Let me help," Ethan said.

So much for quick and simple.

Whatever last hopes of a quick and simple unloading disappeared as soon as Nikolas put those flowers into Ethan's arms. I hadn't minded having a new delivery person earlier, especially with seeing April's reaction to Nikolas, but now I was really beginning to miss Anton.

He never would have made the same mistake. I made a mental note to call the wholesaler and ask about him.

Before I could blow a fuse, April appeared, stacking her box of geraniums on top of the box Ethan was already holding, forcing him to take a step back in order to regain his balance.

"They go inside on the work table," she ordered before giving me a satisfied smile.

April had gotten the wrong idea entirely. No way was I going to let Ethan help us unload our flowers, with what had happened the previous night.

I snatched the top box from Ethan, setting it on the ground. I had to nip this in the bud before it got any further.

"We don't need your help," I snapped.

April watched this, caught the gist, and then followed my lead, snatching the remaining box in Ethan's arms, as if she hadn't just handed him one. "That's right, we don't need your help!"

She proceeded to deliver her best evil eye to him.

Ethan did his best to avoid it, shifting slightly in place. It was irritating how even in an awkward situation, Ethan somehow made it look good.

I tried to figure out the most efficient way to get rid of him.

Nikolas broke the brief silence. "There are more flowers so…" He let the sentence trail as he turned to jog back across the alley to the truck.

Ethan took a step, making to follow Nikolas, when I grabbed his arm, stopping him. If he was determined to help us, I'd have to drag out the interaction for God knows how long. Plus, then I'd feel indebted to him for his help, which meant a much longer conversation.

No, I had to bite the bullet and get this over with. The sooner he was out of our hair, the better

I shooed April away to continue with the unloading and led Ethan down the back alley, away from the shop's back door so we could have some privacy. He picked up the two coffees from the ground and followed.

I took a breath, steeling myself, putting on my best shopkeeper face, then turned to Ethan. "If you're unhappy with the bouquet you purchased yesterday, then we'll be more than happy to make you a replacement, or give you a refund if you return during our regular hours."

Hopefully that would make it clear to him that I wanted no part in his silly games.

Ethan started to say something when a car honked, surprising us both. We both stepped aside, closer to the wall, and let the small black sedan drive past.

When it was gone, we stood in silence.

I couldn't bring myself to repeat myself, and if he hadn't gotten the message already, then I'd probably need a very large stick to beat him over the head with.

Unfortunately, there weren't any large sticks lying around in the alley.

Ethan stepped over a puddle of questionable liquid that seeped out from a nearby dumpster and looked at me pointedly.

"Not quite Lake Goldwater," Ethan said. His voice sounded somber, almost reverent.

I opened my mouth to shoot off something snarky, but fell short.

Lake Goldwater. The mention of the woods where we used to play pulled at something deep in my chest. I remembered the cool shade of the woods, the rustling thicket, the sounds of chickadees chirping, the smell of the sun hitting the leaves, the golden afternoon sun glinting off of the still water.

It'd been so long since I thought about that place, that now it almost seemed like a dream. Did that place really exist or had it just been a fantasy? A hidden spot in the woods where Mother Nature had sheltered us from the world and its senseless cruelty. It seemed too good to be true.

We were so young...and so foolish.

If Ethan had intended to disarm me by mentioning Lake Goldwater, it was working, despite my best intentions to stay upset. It was difficult to hold on to my anger when I felt transported away to the only time in my childhood that I remembered as being truly joyful.

Finally, I took a deep breath and crossed my arms, looking at him wryly.

"I certainly wouldn't recommend kicking your shoes off and walking around barefoot," I said, glancing at a smashed beer bottle near the brick wall. "And if you see any yellow in the puddles, that definitely isn't gold."

Ethan followed my gaze, smiled and nodded, his eyes distant, lost himself in some memory. "It's been some time, Sierra."

I didn't respond, instead studying my shoes, letting the silence extend, letting the minutes tick by, wondering how much time I would really need before I could face Ethan again, before the recent past could fade into distant memory.

"We're a long way from the woods," Ethan said.

"We're not kids anymore," I said, in agreement. Somehow, though I hadn't intended to, it felt like we had synced up, matching our internal tempos. It felt strangely natural and comfortable, like I was returning home.

"Well," Ethan said, breaking me out of my reverie, "I still like to kick my shoes off and feel the grass under my feet."

I raised my eyebrows at him. Mr. Thorne, billionaire CEO playboy, feeling the grass under his feet? The image seemed preposterous, but Ethan smiled back, and for some reason I believed him.

This was more of the Ethan I remembered. How many Ethan Thornes were there? And which one had I met that night at the Conservation Fund event? The night we let ourselves get carried away. The night we got into this mess. I had to know. I had to ask.

"That night," I started, speaking quickly before I could lose my nerve, "if you knew who I was the entire time, why didn't you say anything?"

Ethan thought about it, his brow furrowed. His dark eyes flickered back and forth, before he looked back up at me, his gaze intense, questioning but without malice. "Why didn't you?"

I didn't know what to say. No convincing lie was forthcoming and the truth was too frightening to speak aloud.

Because I wanted to learn about the person you had become without revealing myself to you.

I wanted to see you, without you seeing me.

I studied Ethan's expression but his face was inscrutable.

Perhaps we shared similar reasons for doing what we did.

And perhaps that was why we felt that instant connection. But that connection had transformed into something else that night, something more intense and needy, darker and more powerful, a sexual energy that had burned so hot that it frightened me to the core.

"That night—"

Ethan cut me off, "That night we were picking cards from different decks, playing our hands sloppily, out of turn, and under different rules."

"And what about last night?"

The night when he'd asked about the ribbon, the slip of fabric he'd tied sensually around my ankle, marking me, making my skin nearly burn with sensation. There was no mistaking his meaning when he brought up the ribbon.

"I'm not here about that," Ethan said, quicker than I had anticipated.

So he really was here just to…talk? To catch up? To treat those earlier mistakes like they didn't really happen? To act like the adults we needed to be?

Maybe I'd gotten it backwards, maybe this was us returning to a state of childlike innocence, when we still believed that good triumphed over evil and that true love was right around the corner.

Nikolas's truck started, rumbling for a moment, before rolling away, jouncing out the other end of the alley, leaving Ethan and I alone.

April must've finished unloading already. How long had I been out here talking to Ethan?

For some strange reason, I didn't feel in a hurry to return to the shop, or to prep the flowers anymore.

Something between us had shifted and we both sensed it.

"So," I began, a smile curling at the corner of my mouth, "if you're not here about *that*, you must *really* want that refund then."

Ethan chuckled, his soft smile returning. "How about a do over?" he asked, offering me one of the coffees.

I lifted my hand to the cup reflexively, then hesitated. "The last time I accepted a drink from you…"

"Never happened."

I watched him suspiciously, but he really seemed to mean it.

"Well then," I said, accepting the drink, "I could use a real cup of coffee."

The cup was still warm in my hand.

"Oh," Ethan said, as if he'd forgotten something, searching his pockets with his free hand. "I wasn't sure how you took your coffee, so…" He pulled out a couple of sugar packets and creamers and offered them to me.

Through the fog of time, I remembered a faint image of Ethan, offering me a beetle that he'd found, all shimmery purple and metallic green, six spindly legs clinging to his hand. As much of a tomboy as I was as a kid, it'd freaked me out, and I had shrieked, terrified, making Ethan drop the bug.

Something about the way he stretched out his hand had triggered the memory, one that I'd long forgotten.

"I like my coffee black," I said, taking a sip.

"I'll remember that," he said, taking a sip of his coffee, mirroring me.

The way he said it made it sound like a contract.

Ethan Thorne would remember that I take my coffee black.

That meant something, perhaps.

The coffee was strong and good. Not exactly like how I liked to make it in the mornings, but a solid choice. Apparently having good taste in coffee was something that we shared. It made me wonder if there were other things that we might still have in common, even after all these years.

It was uncanny but it almost felt like Ethan had the exact same thought at that exact same moment.

"So, what are you doing Saturday night?"

"Are you asking me to dinner?" I asked playfully, acting more surprised than I should have been.

"Well," Ethan said, "asking you to coffee would be a bit redundant wouldn't it?"

It made chuckle. Sometimes history repeated itself, and every time I accepted a drink from Ethan, it always led to more complications. This time, however, I welcomed those complications. I was going with the flow, taking things slowly, one step at a time.

I took a step closer to Ethan, pulling the pen I had clipped to my shirt off, and then scribbled my number onto the top of his coffee cup.

"Don't surprise me," I said pointedly, before returning to the shop.

Playing Dress Up

"My poor, poor Billy Reston had two left feet," April said. She lifted her head up in the air, amused, a smile on her face, before grabbing one of the many dresses on my bed and presenting me with a sequined, frilly body hugger that I couldn't recall purchasing.

"Veto," I replied, shaking my head at my past self for thinking that I could pull that off. "Well, *my* prom date was James...Armitage," I struggled with remembering the last name. "He was more than happy to abandon me whenever he could to stand in the middle of the dance floor, performing hip hop moves like a very stiff robot. That's what I get for picking the first guy who asked me to prom. He was almost as poor of a choice as the decision to buy that hideous dress."

April tossed the dress and hanger back onto my bed and propped her hands against her hips. "Well, we've gone through your entire closet Nev, you *have* to pick *something*."

"But do I though?"

She raised an eyebrow. "I suppose you could go naked. Very daring."

I couldn't hold back a snort at that one.

April sighed and gave me the look. The one that said that I was being unreasonable, which maybe in a sense I was. It'd been a few days since I agreed to a date with Ethan, a few days to sit and squirm and try to talk myself out of it, that nagging voice in the back of my mind trying to outline all the different ways in which it might turn out poorly.

Though, to be fair, trading stories with April about our disastrous high school prom dates reminded me that no matter how bad this upcoming date with Ethan *might* turn out, there was no way in hell it could beat the awkward stumbling of that adolescent courtship ritual.

I picked up the red dress, simple and form fitting, with a cowl neck. I couldn't remember the last time I'd worn this number. I had bought it at a department store sale, but somehow the dressing room lighting always seemed to flatter while the light in the real world never did. It was very possible I'd only worn it once.

"Maybe this one," I said, sliding it on over my head.

April looked at me in the mirror and gawked at me. "I told you Nev, you look *gorgeous* in that! You sure you don't need a chaperone? I'd pay good money to see his face when he spots you in that."

I looked in the mirror. I'd gotten the dress when I was thinner, so I hadn't been expecting much, but somehow, I'd gained weight in just the right places to fill out the dress. It was a bit tighter than I would have liked, and the low cut neckline seemed a little too excited to show off my breasts, so I wasn't totally comfortable, but I did look pretty good.

"Thanks April," I said, "appreciate the confidence boost."

"I'm serious! You look *hot*," she said, fanning herself with her hand which earned an eye roll from me.

"I dunno, April."

"That's definitely the dress to wear, Nev, trust me."

Resigned to the dubious fate of me and the red dress, I didn't put up a fuss.

April continued, "Now, let's talk jewelry."

Luckily my options were limited having already chosen a dress, and I ended up with a choice between a set of matching pearls and gold hoops. After much consideration, I finally went with the pearls, with only a few minutes to spare.

Ethan had said that he would pick me up at six o'clock. He struck me as the type to be punctual, and I didn't want to be the kind of woman to make him wait, having dealt with enough events that started late in my professional life to know how annoying that was.

So as expected, my doorbell rang at exactly six.

"Okay, you can lock up for me right?" I asked anxiously.

"Will you stop worrying and just go already?" April said, dangling her set of keys to my apartment in front of me. "I've got everything covered. Besides, I gotta mooch off your Netflix subscription while I still can. Now shoo! Go and have fun! "

I gave April one last hug, taking deep breaths to calm the butterflies in my stomach.

Different Times

A sleek, shiny black town car was parked on the street right in front of my apartment building. The driver, a portly Filipino man, stood in front wearing a sharp black suit that matched the car.

He walked over.

"You must be Ms. Kinsey, a pleasure to meet you," he said, shaking my hand politely. "My name is Emanuel Bautista, please call me Manny," he continued, pointing to the gold plated name tag on his lapel, "I will be your driver tonight."

"Oh," I said, confused. "Is Ethan waiting in the car?"

"Mr. Thorne wishes to express his deepest apologies. He is occupied with a few last minute obligations, so he will be meeting you at dinner."

I'd expected Ethan at my door so that I could get my jitters over with, but I suppose I'd have to wait a bit longer. He had mentioned after all that he was in L.A. on business. This was just one of the things I'd have to learn to get used to if I wanted to date Ethan.

The driver opened the backseat door for me, and I thanked him as I slid awkwardly inside. I was careful not to bump my head, trying to remember how to walk properly in skinny stiletto heels while also being watchful of the neckline of the red dress. I wasn't exactly used to having my doors opened for me, but Manny, a perfect professional, acted as if he didn't even notice my clumsy clambering.

The interior of the car was furnished in a light tan leather, and I sank into the seats, clutching my purse in front of me like a talisman, trying not to let my anxiety get the better of me.

We drove in silence as Manny took us onto the freeway which, though busy, was moving along smoothly today. The butterflies in my stomach reminded me of when I'd first started Venus Floral Design and really had to network to get business for the shop.

Sucking in a breath, I knew I had to start talking just to get out of my own head. We still had the entire ride before I met Ethan, and I wasn't about to let the anxiety seep deep into my bones before I'd even gotten out of the car.

"So, how long have you worked for Ethan?" I asked as relaxed as I could manage.

Manny chuckled, dropping the stiff formality of before. "Oh, a good minute," he said, eyes brightening in the rearview mirror as he flashed me a look, restrained but friendly. "Maybe seven years or so at this point, I'd say."

Seven years. Practically half of the long fifteen years that Ethan and I had lost track of each other.

Something in my chest clenched tighter.

Manny must have known so much about Ethan, the type of person he was, the things that he preferred, the things he worried about, the things he cared about. There was so much I wanted to ask, but my throat clenched, constricted by the overwhelming weight of history.

"Do you enjoy working for him?" I asked, trying to keep my questions light and innocent.

Manny smiled at me through the rearview mirror, the crows feet around his eyes deepening. He looked like a man used to laughing heartily.

"Are you trying to get me to lose my job?" he asked teasingly.

I laughed louder than I'd expected which helped to dissipate some of my nervous energy. In that instance, I adored Manny immensely. He was so laid back and easy to talk to that it was really helping me get out of my own head.

"I don't know, could you tell me any secrets that would cost you your job?" I asked dramatically. "Late night rendezvous, secret affairs? Anything you think that I might need to know on my first date with your boss?"

Manny shook his head, grinning. "You really think Mr. Thorne is like that?"

I took a moment, considering it.

Did I really think Ethan was like that?

After turning my head to look out the window, I confessed what felt like the truth. "I'm not really sure I know what Ethan is like at all."

Manny went quiet and I couldn't help wondering if I'd somehow offended him, but after a few moments, he answered, "He's a good boss, always treats me right, but...Mr. Thorne...he's a complicated man, it wouldn't be my place to speak for him."

I nodded and settled back into my seat. He was right. As tempting as it was, it wasn't right of me to pry Manny for information that I could very well discover for myself when I met Ethan.

It did reflect well on Ethan though to have such a cool driver. Did Manny joke around with Ethan too? Did Ethan joke back? What was his sense of humor like? I exhaled slowly and looked back out the window at the passing cars on the interstate. There was still so much I wanted to know.

After a few minutes, Manny shifted in his seat, maybe sensing my curiosity or unease and added, "It's just like any other job, you know."

I caught his gaze through the rearview and raised an eyebrow. "Driving around a billionaire is hardly like any other job."

Manny chuckled. "It's not what you're imagining. I take Mr. Thorne from Point A to Point B, and then I sit in my car at Point B until him and his assistant are done with their meeting, then we return to Point A. Occasionally we go to Point C."

"Scandalous," I teased, glad that Manny was still happy to chat more. "By his assistant, you mean Nicole?"

"Ah, you've already met her."

"I've seen her around," I said offhandedly, not wanting to get into the details of the night I'd met Ethan again, suddenly reminded of what hiding from Nicole had led us to.

Since Manny had mentioned that he didn't want to divulge too much about his boss, I changed the topic, so as not to put him in an awkward position.

"Do you drive anyone else, Manny?" I asked.

"Well," Manny thought to himself, then continued, "Back before Mr. Thorne hired me, I used to drive for a company and the rich folk that I picked up hardly said a single word to me, you'd think they'd never heard the words 'Please' and 'Thank You' before either." He shook his head like he was shaking his finger at a young child. "That was ages ago though."

Manny made a wide left with the car before looking at me again through the rearview mirror. "Mr. Thorne says you're an old friend, Ms. Kinsey. How old, if you don't mind me asking?"

It was an innocent question, and I felt some obligation to answer truthfully considering how forthright Manny had been with my questions.

"Very old," I said. "Probably about fifteen years give or take."

"Ah," Manny replied like something had clicked in his mind before clearing his throat. "That is a very long time."

It was a long time indeed. I nodded in agreement but didn't say anything.

"You know," Manny continued, "when Ethan was starting up Thorne Engines, I used to pick up a lot of folks for him from the airport. And Ethan would always talk my ear off about a lot of technical stuff that I could barely understand, but I was happy to listen. It was a different time. He was busier, but he seemed happier. Yeah, different times…"

Manny trailed off, seemingly deep in thought, and I breathed quietly, trying to hold on to the scraps of Ethan's life that I was hearing, not daring to interrupt in case Manny stopped talking.

Before I could figure out what to ask or if it was even appropriate to ask Manny for more, the GPS on the dashboard announced robotically:

In a quarter-mile, keep right. You will be arriving at your destination.

Outside the window, I could see that we'd made it to the Hollywood strip with its bright glaring lights, the Chinese theatre on the left, and the costumed superheroes that hustled tourists for money.

The car slowed as we pulled into a side street, pulling to a stop in front of a blank grey door with a small gilded sign above the doorway that read: "Avante"

Manny cleared his throat again, startling me out of my thoughts.

"Come to think of it," Manny said, "other than Ethan and his assistant, you're the only other person that I've driven for Ethan in a long, long time."

Avante

When the car door opened, I was immediately smacked in the face with the noise of honking horns from the bumper to bumper traffic, buskers blaring their music on portable speakers, and the sheer mass of humanity, hoping to catch a glimpse of their favorite celebrity.

I accepted Manny's offered hand to help me out of the car, and this time, I managed the transition with a little more grace. Though we were a full block away from the main Hollywood strip, the cacophony from the busiest street in L.A. still managed to travel the distance.

The noise did little to drown out the questions that were bouncing around in my head: What had changed about Ethan since Manny first drove for him? Why was I the first person that Manny had driven in a while? Why had Manny told me that?

Still unsettled, I said goodbye to Manny, walked up to the door of *Avante*, fixed my dress, making sure everything was where it was supposed to be and squashed down the questions bubbling in my mind.

There was no reason to jump the gun, to know everything there was to know about Ethan right away. Ethan and I were about to have a nice date, learn about each other without any expectations, and have a good time. Nothing to get all twisted up about.

When I was satisfied that I was ready, I took a deep breath and stepped inside *Avante.*

To absolute silence.

The restaurant had somehow managed to suck all the sounds from the street like a powerful vacuum. I felt like I had been teleported into an entirely different world––a world I wasn't entirely prepared for.

My heart beat wildly as my senses tried to catch up to the jarring change of setting. I swallowed hard and blinked rapidly to adjust to the intimate low lighting of the restaurant in time to observe thirty or so heads swiveling back to their dinners.

Of course, the door opening had drawn everyone's attention.

It felt like I'd stepped into church right as the preacher was delivering a sermon on modesty.

Not exactly the entrance I wanted to make.

Instinctively, I brought my purse up to my chest, to cover my cleavage, my cheeks heating up a few degrees. I knew I never should have let April talk me into wearing this dress.

Now I felt like a cheap hooker at a Christmas sermon. My red dress stood out, blaring against the monochromatic theme of the restaurant. I wondered if the patrons had all decided to coordinate with the decor with nobody standing out in particular.

The restaurant had a surprising amount of floor space, but the small tables, covered with a bone-white tablecloth, were scattered about, making room instead for a variety of large avant-garde art installations. In contrast to the rather bland decor, the art looked like an emo unicorn had thrown up dark-gray rainbows into a variety of sculpted towering pieces, splotches and swirls making their way from the floor to the ceiling. Small glass bulbs were hung from the ceiling with fishing lines, each filled with varying quantities of black liquid.

The centerpiece was a giant flat aquarium standing in the middle of the room, separating the kitchen from the dining area.

It was filled with pulsating white jellyfish.

I never felt so out of place as I did at the entrance of that restaurant. The other patrons of the restaurant were nearly silent, whispering to each other. Occasionally, I could hear the soft tinkle of silverware against plate, and if I strained my ears, I could barely make out soft melody being played from a harpsichord at the corner of the restaurant.

Was I really in the right place?

A thin, tall man, dressed in a zebra patterned tuxedo, with a severe nose and platinum hair that looked like it belonged in a science fiction film, hurried over and greeted me. "You must be Ms. Kinsey, please, right this way to your table."

Even that sounded like it was whispered.

I nodded and followed the man. My heels clicked loudly in the muted room, and I quickly leaned forward, relying on the balls of my feet to teeter more quietly over to the table, trying to adapt to the hushed environment. I kept my eyes on the ground, hoping that if I didn't look at anyone else in the restaurant, it would make me immune to any glances as well.

Besides, I needed to watch my feet anyway, to make sure I didn't tip over onto my face.

"Mr. Thorne," I heard the man say as he approached a table. "Your guest."

I looked up to see Ethan, wearing a slim black suit, stand from the table as our eyes met. Seeing him filled me with a strange heady mixture of attraction and relief. Somehow, Ethan managed to have an air of ease and control, even in an outlandish environment like this.

Ethan's eyes took me in, subtly, but noticeably.

"You look lovely tonight," he said.

"Thank you," I said, blushing slightly at his compliment, fighting the urge to curtsey.

"Please," Ethan said, motioning his hand, palm up to my chair.

The maitre'd pulled my chair out as Ethan gracefully sat down in sync with me. I cringed when the feet of the chair squeaked against the floor as the maitre'd helped scooch it under me.

Then he floated away, leaving me alone with Ethan.

"I must apologize for not picking you up personally," Ethan said. "I hope that the ride wasn't too much trouble."

"Oh no, not at all." I smiled tightly, self-conscious of the volume of my voice. "Your driver was excellent, thank you for sending him," I said.

Ethan nodded, as if he'd expected nothing less.

We looked at each other for a moment, neither of us saying anything, letting the silence extend just long enough to make it awkward. The nerves that had melted away during the easy conversation with Manny were brought back twofold after entering this bizarre restaurant, and now, those pesky nerves were about to spill out all over the place trying to talk to Ethan.

Come on Sierra, you got this!
I started, "So—"
"I—"

"I'm sorry," I said, "You go first."

"No, please, you have nothing to apologize for."

"We could have rescheduled if you had a work obligation."

Ethan waved it away. "It was nothing, just a difficult negotiation that went overtime. I'm glad you could make it."

"Yes, me too," I replied, my stiff smile continuing to have trouble relaxing.

We looked at each other.

Perfect, off to a thrilling start.

We hadn't even had appetizers yet and it seemed like we had already run out of things to talk about. Exactly what every woman dreamt of when they fantasized about dinner with the most eligible bachelor on the Forbes List.

I had to pull myself together.

I took a few deep breaths as slowly as I could, but the tightening waistband of the dress didn't make it easy and my rigid posture had yet to relax. Fortunately, my breaths did manage to buy me enough time to gather my thoughts.

An unfamiliar environment didn't mean that everything I knew about conversation went out the window. Plus, I still wanted to learn more about Ethan. Even if Ethan proved to be a hard nut to crack, it was only a first date, and I was confident in my skills at small talk. A few years of having to network aggressively to land gigs for the flower shop had made sure of that. And if there was one thing I learned, it was that entrepreneurs always loved talking about their startup days.

Keeping a cheery disposition, I said, "Your driver tells me that he's been driving for you since you started your company."

"Oh? Is that what he said?" Ethan fixed me with his gaze, guarded, betraying nothing, like I was sitting across from him at the negotiation table. But there was a problem: It wasn't clear what we were negotiating.

The waiter, thankfully, interrupted us. The thin gaunt man was dressed in a white robe that reminded me of a monk's habit, and I would have taken a closer look if my attention hadn't been quickly drawn to the large intricate bird's nest adornment, made of varying sizes of wires, on top of his head.

As soon as my eyes flicked away to stop myself from staring, the waiter expertly set two long leaf-shaped plates onto the table. I looked down to see two small saucers filled with dipping sauces, resting on the larger leaf-shaped plate, along with a long thin-handled teaspoon.

The waiter announced, "These are your starters. The soup on your left is 'the black ocean,' with a black sesame base, and the soup on your right is 'waves hitting the beach,' which is our house bisque."

He bowed politely before leaving us.

Apparently, they *weren't* dipping sauces.

But I had bigger fish to fry right now than unraveling the culinary mysteries before me.

Picking the conversation back up, I continued, "Manny mentioned that things have changed a lot since—"

"You are on a first name basis with my driver already?" Ethan raised his eyebrows at me, his face inscrutable.

"Uh," the word got tangled in my throat at the sudden interruption, "well, he seemed to want me to call him by name." I forced a chuckle, unsure of how exactly to respond to the question and waved my hand dismissively. "Anyways, it must have been a challenging time when you started the business. What was it like?"

"It was…" Ethan nodded slowly, tilting his head to the side. "Difficult…as you said."

I mirrored him, nodding enthusiastically, making eye contact, trying to encourage him to continue.

"Shall we?" Ethan asked, looking toward the saucers on the table.

I kept nodding stupidly until I realized he wanted to start eating already.

"Ah yes, of course," I said, feeling my cheeks flush.

So much for that.

The soup was finished within a couple of spoonfuls, and neither Ethan nor I had said another word. The awkwardness was unbearable; it felt as if I was holding my breath.

The rest of the dinner wasn't much better, but Ethan did begin to ask me some questions about how I'd gotten into the flower business, and we exchanged pleasantries and small talk for far longer than I could imagine enduring. The fact that we had to whisper for the majority of our conversation did little to help things along. It was perfectly polite, though Ethan seemed distant, preoccupied, and cold.

When dinner was over, I was glad to finally get out of there.

We exited *Avante*, and the sounds of the street filled me with a feeling of vitality and relief. It reminded me that there was an entire world outside where we didn't have to whisper.

We walked the few short steps to Manny, who was waiting to take us back to our respective homes.

"Welcome back," Manny said, smiling pleasantly at the both of us before opening the door of the town car.

I was happy to see his jovial face again and reflexively mirrored a pleasant smile in return.

"Thank you, Manny," I said.

At least I wouldn't have to hold my breath in that pretentious restaurant anymore. But the moment I ducked my head into the car, it was silent once again.

Ethan slid into the backseat beside me, eyes facing forward.

It was going to be a *long* drive back.

What the hell had happened to our chemistry? Our connection? Which Ethan was I interacting with now? The Ethan that wanted to try again or the surly CEO?

I racked my mind trying to figure out what had gone wrong. It felt like I had known Ethan better when he had come to the shop to ask for this date, coffees in hand. Or even during that first night we met at the Conservation Fund event. We hadn't been upfront with each other but at least I would have preferred the games that we played over *this* wooden formality.

Ethan turned to me, his face impassive. "I hope dinner was satisfactory," he said.

"Oh yes, thank you Ethan, it was delicious," I lied, tucking my purse into my lap. Though the food was rather interesting, all of the portions were in the same vein as the tiny saucer of soup, and I wasn't close to feeling at all well satiated.

Manny shut the door gently, deepening the silence in the cabin of the car.

My stomach, as if on cue, grumbled loudly.

Very loudly.

Too loudly to politely ignore.

Before I could even manage to get embarrassed, I heard another equally loud grumble, this time coming from Ethan.

We looked at each other for a beat, neither of us sure of what to do, neither of us willing to call the other out on our little white lies, neither of us willing to acknowledge the obvious truth.

The tension built and built until it was too much for us to bear and we both burst out in laughter.

Ethan roared with mirth, peals of his laughter mixing in with mine, making a symphony inside the cabin, loud and authentic.

When I got control of myself again, my sides hurt from laughing so hard. I said, "I really do appreciate you taking me to dinner." Not wanting to sound ungrateful, I added, "It was a very unique venue. I don't think I've ever been anywhere like it."

Ethan wiped his eyes, his shoulders still shaking. "The decor was awfully gloomy and it was as quiet as a funeral in there. Not exactly what I'd expected..."

"Wait, you haven't eaten there before?"

Ethan shrugged. "It came recommended. I'm often too busy to eat at sit down places, myself."

"Well, it was an interesting experience, and —"

"No, no," Ethan cut in. "We're well past the bullshit now."

I quieted. "Okay, fine. It was…uncomfortable," I said before giggling.

Ethan sighed deeply and shook his head, "I really should apologize. First, for not picking you up in person, and then taking you to *that* dreadful place. I had no idea that it was going to be like that."

Manny, who had gotten himself settled in the front, looked at us from the rearview mirror. "Where to boss?" he asked.

Instead of answering right away, Ethan turned to me. "I've completely screwed up. I'll understand if you'd prefer to return home right away but since we're both still hungry, would you be willing to give me a second chance?"

Ethan was smiling, his face animated and genuine. It was more of the Ethan I remembered. The Ethan that made me want to act more like myself.

"That depends," I gave him a smirk, "are we going to a place lit only with candles where the waiters dress in flowing black capes like Count Dracula?"

Ethan chuckled. "Only if that's what you're into."

"Definitely not."

"Good, me neither." Ethan pulled his phone out of his jacket pocket. "I have a list of recommendations for the trendiest places in L.A. from —"

Before I could catch myself, I grabbed Ethan's forearm.

Ethan looked at me surprised.

"How about we go somewhere where we can both be comfortable. Maybe something a little more casual?" I suggested, not wanting a slightly different version of *Avante*.

"Of course." Ethan slipped his phone back into his pocket, and thought to himself before looking forward to Manny. "Do you have any suggestions Manny?"

Manny readjusted himself in his seat and looked back into the mirror at Ethan. "There is one place, though it has been awhile…" Manny trailed off, the uncertainty clear in his voice.

"Oh," Ethan said rather flatly.

I looked between Ethan and Manny. Ethan must have known exactly the place that Manny was referring to, but didn't seem too keen on the suggestion. I wondered just what their history was with it. Whatever it was, my curiosity was piqued.

Ethan looked at me and I couldn't hold back a rather puzzled look in return, but he stared at me for a beat longer than I was expecting, causing a flush to rise to my cheeks. He then blinked back to Manny, loosened his tie, and took a deep audible breath.

"Alright Manny, take us to El Gran Guererro."

El Gran Guererro

El Gran Guererro was everything that Avante was not.

In fact, El Gran Guererro wasn't even a restaurant.

Manny had driven us to an empty parking lot with plastic lawn chairs scattered across weed stricken asphalt. There was cheerful guitar music playing from a stereo somewhere close by. A line of college students, well dressed professionals, as well as the occasional construction worker wearing neon yellow t-shirts and scuffed work boots, snaked its way across the lot to a brightly painted taco truck.

I was pretty sure this degree of casualness was the cause of Ethan's initial hesitation, but it was exactly the kind of environment in which I could imagine standing with April and waiting in line together. The festive environment felt very comfortable for me, but how did a man like Ethan know about a place like this?

More importantly, was Ethan showing me his true self or just what he thought I wanted to see?

The sun had set, and the cool breeze of the evening had started sashaying through the concrete corridors of L.A., brushing the heat off my face and making the hairs on my skin stand. Ethan had taken off his jacket and placed it gently on my shoulders when we made the walk over to the taco truck's line.

Even from the back of the line we could smell the delicious aromas of spice and grilled meats wafting through the night air. After the pretentious surreality of Avante, it was refreshing to be here.

I turned to Ethan and said, "Let me guess, you come here for the tacos after you've had your fill of five-hundred dollar Scotches."

"Not exactly..." he said.

Ethan had unbuttoned the first two buttons of his shirt and let his loosened tie hang freely. The gel that had held his hair earlier was softening and his hair tousled around carelessly, adding to his just-off-work laid back image. The mellow look gave him a more approachable charming vibe, and I felt the butterflies making laps around my stomach, sending desire fluttering in my heart.

A gruff voice came from the front of the line, "Senor Thorne!"

We both looked over to see that the voice belonged to a gray-bearded Mexican elderly man—a very jolly, rosy cheeked, round faced man—taking orders from the window. "Get out of the line mijo, what do you think are you doing?"

He spoke some rapid fire Spanish to the cooks behind him in the truck, and someone took off their gloves to replace him.

The old man opened the side door, yanked his apron off, hung it on the door knob, then clambered down the steps, walked over to us, and, without missing a beat, scooped Ethan up in a giant bear hug.

I looked cautiously between Ethan and the man, who might as well have been a perfect Mexican Santa, trying to figure out exactly what the nature of their relationship was. They seemed like old friends, but the man was much older than Ethan.

"Not enough meat still, unlike me!" The man laughed, rubbing his large belly, and then the man turned his attention to me, a wide dimpled grin on his face, "And you brought a guest! A lady guest! How can you make your guest wait in line like that? Ay! Rude!"

The man grabbed my hand with both of his and shook excitedly. "I am Guererro, everyone calls me *Mister* Guerrero," he winked at me, "pleased to meet you!"

"It's a pleasure to meet you, Mr. Guerrero, I'm Sierra," I replied in a similar attitude of excitement. It was hard not to want to be equally friendly with such a friendly person.

Mr. Guererro looked from me to Ethan a couple of times and I suddenly felt embarrassed that maybe he was assuming we were boyfriend and girlfriend. Something about the assumption made me feel like a teenage girl all over again.

"Wonderful, wonderful, to see you both," he said before turning his attention to Ethan. "We must catch up later sometime, for now, you must want the best tacos in L.A., no?"

"Of course," Ethan said, "but I didn't want to cut in front of the other customers."

Mr. Guererro scoffed, then quickly squinted at Ethan. "The customers? Without you, there would be no customers!" He laughed heartily, his belly jiggling along. "You two, sit, sit, aqui," he said, pulling out a small foldable table from the back of the truck, as well as two matching foldable seats, and opened it with practiced hands. He smacked the surface of the table with his hand a few times signaling us to sit and enjoy.

We both sat close enough for our knees to bump into each other, and I gave Ethan a questioning look after Mr. Guererro had stepped back into the taco truck. It was hard to imagine Ethan setting up this entire scene as a ruse. Slowly, I was getting used to the idea that maybe, just maybe I was seeing the true Ethan. Except now, I felt like I had more questions than before. And what exactly had Mr. Guererro meant when he said that there would be no customers without Ethan?

Ethan looked at me, smiling pleasantly but not volunteering anything either.

"Are you really going to make me ask?"

He shrugged, "Can't a man keep his secrets?"

As much as I wanted to learn more about Ethan, just seeing him more relaxed and like himself was enough for now. I could bask in the moment, there would be plenty of time for questions later.

"Their Al Pastor tacos really are the best in Los Angeles," Ethan continued.

"I believe you."

"You do?" Ethan looked at me a bit surprised like perhaps he had presumed that I wouldn't have let him get away with changing the subject.

"I do. It smells delicious!"

Ethan leaned back, getting settled into the small chair and grinned, "Prepare to be impressed then."

The tacos came out on red and white checkered paper trays, delivered by Mr. Guererro personally. The jolly man also set down two beers in front of us, each with a small wedge of lime stuck inside the mouth.

"So why'd you take me to *Avante* if this is where you really like to eat?" I asked.

Ethan shrugged. "Guess we both have trouble taking our masks off."

I clinked my beer bottle against his, "To masks, then," and took a drink.

Ethan and I munched on the tacos and they were indeed heavenly, juicy and savory with the right amount of citrus to balance everything out. I found it easy to ask Ethan about his love of tacos and other taco places he tried in L.A. When we fell into companionable silence, we alternated between sipping our beers and watching the crowd. At some point, an impromptu dance party had broken out next to the stereo system.

I watched Mr. Guererro deliver a tray of tacos to Manny. The two hugged, rubbed each other's bellies like a couple of jokesters, and had a laugh together, like old buddies.

"You both must have been real regulars, huh?" I asked Ethan, motioning to them.

Ethan nodded and finished the last of his beer before speaking. "Earlier, you asked me about the early days of my company. Well, I spent most of them traveling back and forth between L.A. and Silicon Valley. I'd often get into town very late, I still had to eat, and hotel food is just dreadful."

"So what you're saying," I said, playfully, "is that the true power behind Thorne Engines is Al Pastor tacos?"

"Purely off the record."

"That doesn't exactly explain why you and Mr. Guererro are so close, unless you expect me to believe this is the same treatment all regulars get," I said.

"A few years ago, Mr. Guererro ran into some financial difficulties, so I made a small investment into his truck." Ethan's eyes caught a reflection of one of the festive hanging lights, and for a moment, I wondered how I ever saw the coldness in him.

"Seems like that was a good business decision," I said, nodding toward the crowd.

"I suppose I've made a few," Ethan said, with a modest shrug.

There was a sensation of something pulling deep within my chest and before I knew it I was moving, closing the distance toward him.

We kissed, both of us still smelling of grilled pork and limes.

Ethan put his arm around my waist to pull me in closer and we stayed like that for a while longer.

When we broke apart, Ethan had a playful look in his eye.

"I had this whole excursion planned out, you know," Ethan said with a mischievous lilt in his voice.

"Uh-huh, of course you did," I said, copying the mischievous lilt.

Even if the masks had come off, a little pretend couldn't hurt.

A Safe Place

I quickly stepped into my apartment and closed the door behind me. The resulting wind brushed my face, a welcome cool breeze against my hot cheeks. I couldn't help letting a heavy sigh of relief loudly slip through my lips. Instead of letting my legs buckle underneath me, I let the weight of my purse fall to the ground, regaining my composure. I blinked a few times, finally registering that I must have left the light on in my apartment.

The television too.

But I never left the television on.

The sound of static and soft murmurings grew louder in my ears as my brain started jumping to conclusions. Did someone break into my apartment just to turn on my television? I had to unlock the door to get in so maybe they came in through the window? Maybe somehow up the fire escape?

The hairs on the back of my neck stood erect as I heard someone shuffling.

I figured the element of surprise might be on my side, so I bolted to the bedroom where the television was and screamed something very original at the top of my lungs.

"HEY!"

April shrieked, eyes wide in terror, before falling off the side of my bed.

"Oh my gosh, April! You scared me half to death!"

I had completely forgotten that I left April to lock up my place.

"Nev!" April whined, crumpled into a ball on the floor, on the verge of tears. "Oh, you scared me so bad I think I peed myself." She laughed, wiping her eyes.

"I'm so sorry," I said.

"Well, it's just me watching your Netflix," April said, picking herself up as I walked in for a hug.

"What are you still doing here? I thought you had a dinner date with the roomies."

"Well…" She tapped her lip in thought. "I think I wanted to give them an alone kind of date, you know? Speaking of which, how'd your date go?"

Though we were no longer hugging, I could feel April's spirit nuzzling up to me expectantly.

I hadn't even had a chance to process the date yet myself, and I was still feeling a bit sheepish given the kiss that Ethan and I had just shared so I just said, "It was…nice."

"It was?!" She squeaked in excitement. "I mean, of course it was! After all that hullabaloo and confusion, of course things went well." She seemed to be talking more to herself than to me. "So he uh," she smoothed out her hair and tucked strands behind her ear. "He didn't say anything stupid this time?"

"He was actually kind of distracted, so—"

"Distracted?" She looked at me, a puzzled anguished look. "Like he was ignoring you? Why, that piece of—"

"No no no, April, it worked itself out. The date really was very nice."

"Oh, I see," April collected herself. "So, that's it? Anything more than nice?" She wiggled her eyebrows at me, back to her playful self.

"Nice is good enough, April."

"Oh yeah, of course, I know, but you know uh…"

I knew exactly what she was about to say. Definitely something about fate and the universe aligning for us or something of that nature.

April suddenly shook her head. "No yeah, you're right, nice is good," she agreed, nodding. She twisted her body a bit and gave me a shy look. "So… when's the next date?"

"We're taking it slow," I mirrored back, drawing out the last word.

"Aww, don't know yet?"

"No, but," I tilted my head in thought, Ethan's kiss still lingering on my lips. "I hope it's soon."

No Worries

Surprisingly, it didn't take Ethan long to contact me for another date a few days later. He didn't tell me where we'd be heading, but he did say that I should "dress comfortably."

So on Saturday morning, dressed in a loose blouse and my favorite denim shorts and black flats, I waited outside my apartment for Ethan to arrive. It was mid afternoon. The sun was shining and the sky was a brilliant shade of baby blue. It was one of those perfect days in L.A. that reminded me of why I'd stayed out here after college.

The nerves I had felt before our first date were gone, and honestly it gave me much more confidence to be wearing something more casual than the slinky red cowl-neck I had on the other night. In fact, I was even excited. The fact that he'd said to "dress comfortably," added to the potential for adventure.

Besides, I could rest easy in the knowledge that our second date couldn't possibly as awkward as the formal dining experience we had on our first outing.

Though, in a way, I was grateful for that little bit of awkwardness, since it only made our kiss at the taco truck feel more special. It hadn't been a kiss of lusty passion, like we'd shared when we were still pretending to be strangers, but something else. Something sweeter. Something I wanted to enjoy regularly.

Ethan opening up to me and acting more like his genuine self filled me with a sense of bittersweet nostalgia.

I wanted to see more of that Ethan.

But if the previous date was any indication, it felt a bit like I might be rolling the dice with the version of Ethan that showed up on any given day. I did my best to shake the worries away. After all, I'd resolved to *go with the flow*, and take things *one day at a time*, hadn't I?

A loud honk startled me. A few yards down the street, a silver compact car sat idling next to the sidewalk. I squinted to see Ethan waving at me from the driver's seat. A sudden rush of embarrassment washed over me. I hadn't even bothered to notice the car since I had assumed that Ethan would arrive in the black Mercedes driven by Manny. Either that or a flashy sports car.

One dinner at a pretentious Hollywood restaurant and I was already becoming some kind of entitled lizard lady?

Pull yourself back to reality, Sierra!

I made a light jog over to the car, opened the passenger side door, and hopped in. I buckled myself in, turning to Ethan.

"Hi Ethan, sorry, I was —"

His lips were suddenly pressed against mine. His hand slid up the side of my neck and behind my head, pulling me in and deepening the kiss. I melted into his embrace, a wet heat coiling between my legs. When Ethan finally pulled away, he licked his lips, sending a shiver up my spine. I would definitely call that *going with the flow.*

"I've missed you, Sierra."

I scoffed playfully, overcoming the pounding in my chest. "It's only been a few days," I said casually, trying to hide the flush in my cheeks.

"Has it?" Ethan asked distractedly, slowly eyeing my legs before taking me all in. "You look good."

"Looking good yourself," I said with a grin. He wore a blue polo shirt and khaki pants, a major contrast to the suit he wore last time. I noticed that his biceps were constrained in the shirt sleeves, which matched the rippling muscles in his forearm as he loosely held the wheel with one hand. I couldn't wipe the grin off my face as I took in his tousled hair and five o'clock shadow. His lips seemed to glisten from the sunlight and his eyes drooped as he watched me, like he was thinking about... something else.

"What a surprise," I said, "I was half-expecting to be picked up by Manny today, with how busy you are."

"No difficult negotiations," he said with a glimmer in his eye, "So it'll be just the two of us. I hope you're not disappointed."

I looked around the cabin of the car, pretending to appraise it. "Let me guess, the Ferrari is in the shop?"

"This one's a rental," Ethan said. "Like it?"

I flicked my hair back, pretending to be posh. "I suppose a girl can get used to this," I said, "but I'm more worried for you. A Toyota Camry doesn't exactly suit your image."

Ethan looked at me in mock offense.

"You don't think I seem reliable and easy to maintain?"

"I'd have to take a peek under the hood," I blurted out.

Ethan chuckled. "Then I eagerly submit," His eyes lingered on my face a moment longer, until I had to turn away so he wouldn't see me blushing. I hadn't intended our date to start off so sexual, but it seemed like it was heading that way all on its own. Being a gentleman, Ethan let the innuendo slide, probably seeing the tips of my ears turn red. We finally took off, away from the curb and down the street.

Ethan was much more casual and relaxed than when I'd met him in *Avante* on our first date, so I would definitely count that as progress. If the rest of the date continued like this, then there was nothing to be worried about.

"So, where are we going?" I asked when we'd made it onto the highway.

Ethan merely tilted his head toward me with a crooked grin, brimming with promise. "You'll see."

Race Day

Ethan's surprise turned out to be both more and less intimidating than I'd imagined. An hour later—which felt even shorter due to the breezy banter we shared on the drive—we arrived at Motorsports Speedway on the outskirts of the city.

It was obvious by the size of the crowds that we'd arrived on a race day.

Ethan merged us into the line of cars trying to get into the parking lot. Judging by the way the parking situation looked, the stands inside the stadium must have been packed. As we drove inside the complex, there were balloons and checkered flags that were mere decoration compared to the large flags that flew majestically in the wind from the top of the large concrete stadium.

We edged closer to the main stadium until I could hear the roar of engines, humming an insistent, high pitched buzz.

"I've never been to a race before," I said, gawking at the crowds as they got out of their cars and streamed toward the box office.

"Good," Ethan said, "then I have low expectations to live up to."

I laughed, flashing him a look. Who would have thought, Ethan Thorne, master of low expectations.

After we finally found a spot, Ethan took something out of his pocket and suddenly slipped it over my head.

I fingered the lanyard and inspected the badge that was attached to the clip, half-expecting to see "VIP" printed on it, but instead saw "STAFF" in capital blue letters.

I looked closer at the name on the tag. "I'm…Amy?" I asked puzzled, before reaching for the tag on the lanyard Ethan had just slipped on himself. "And you're…Todd? You're definitely not a Todd," I said, holding in a laugh.

"I can see you as an Amy," Ethan said.

"How so?"

"It's kind of spunky." He fixed his eyes on me, but I couldn't be sure that he was only looking at my face. "But I guess it is missing that…sultry something," Ethan mused.

"You know, I prefer not to work on my weekends off."

"Work. Play. Sometimes it all blends together. But don't worry, you won't be asked to save the day today. Just relax and follow my lead."

"So that's why you picked up the rental huh? Didn't want to draw too many eyes to a fancy sports car on race day?"

Ethan shrugged and shot me a sly smile. "I did say that alter egos have their uses."

"I'm not even going to get a hint as to why we have staff passes?"

"The wait is half the pleasure," Ethan said, flashing me a cryptic look before stepping out of the car.

I felt a nervous thrill spark through my body. Something about figuring things out on the fly instead of going by a plan made me feel like I was dealing with some last minute disaster at a major event.

I always liked to have things under control and planned out in advance, but Ethan seemed like he had a plan, even if I couldn't tell what it was right now.

Why would Ethan do this? For someone so high profile, I found it difficult to believe that he couldn't just go wherever he wanted whenever he wanted. He wasn't a poor college student sneaking us into a concert.

Though, I suppose the cloak and daggers did give everything an aura of danger and mystery.

I took a few deep breaths before getting myself together and joining Ethan.

Just go with the flow, Sierra.

Instead of the large entrance other patrons were taking, Ethan took us to a metal door that had no label or signage. He easily opened the stiff metal door for me and we walked in. The noises and voices echoed off the concrete walls, reminding me of the locker room at summer camp. My old local recreation center's hallways were filled with that distinct hollow sound. I didn't have the experience of working an event in a large arena like this so it was exciting to watch the real staff hustling and bustling about.

"Should we snag some staff uniforms too?" I asked, eyeing a pile of work aprons on a table, wondering if Ethan had the cachet to get us out of trespassing charges.

Ethan shook his head. "Everyone will be far too busy with the race to bother with us. We're going to walk briskly now, with purpose."

Ethan gave me a wink as he placed his hand on my lower back, guiding me along as we made our way down the corridor and into the main hallway.

We weaved through the crowd of staff members and vendors, who all ignored us, busy with their individual tasks, and Ethan took a nondescript door along one of the walls. There was, again, no signage or any sort of indication as to where the door would lead, but Ethan seemed to know exactly where we were headed. We made our way past a few other corridors and I could hear the sound of speeding cars getting louder the further inside of the building we went.

We arrived at another metal door, with the only sign next to it stating that it was for emergencies and staff only, and Ethan paused, standing in front of it.

I was about to ask if we were lost, but I noticed Ethan's wide smile as he slowly placed his hand on the door's long push bar.

He looked at me excitedly before saying, "It's been a while since I've been back here."

Then Ethan opened the door and I stumbled backward at the sound and blur of a race car zooming past. Ethan took my hand and pulled me out with him until we were both standing in the sun. We were right next to the track, just a few feet away from the cars rushing past us, separated by a concrete barrier and a chain link fence above it.

At this distance, the cars felt much faster than they ever appeared on TV. The rumble of the engines was loud enough to make my teeth chatter. The air had a distinct smell of burnt rubber and hot asphalt, combining together to form a dizzying mix.

The sheer sensations were overwhelming and my instinct was to immediately turn around and head back into the relative safety of the corridor we'd come from.

Instead, before I could hightail it out of there, Ethan wrapped his arms around me, and pressed his lips against my ear. "It's okay, Sierra. Just close your eyes and let yourself melt into the sound. Just listen and wait... Trust me. It's overwhelming and scary at first, I know, but trust me...just wait for that brief moment of stillness within the chaos."

Even though every instinct in my body screamed for me to run away, I stayed.

I closed my eyes, feeling the strength of his arms holding me, compressing against my chest.

And then I heard it, the stillness within the roar.

A single moment of peace even within all of the overwhelming power of the cars on the track.

When I opened my eyes, Ethan's chest was in front of me and I stepped back.

He watched me cautiously, smiling when he saw that I was also smiling.

The noise was no longer so overwhelming, my body learning that I wasn't in any imminent danger. Instead, the rumbles and waves of sound sent a satisfying thrill through my body, shaking out any other thoughts. Since Ethan was standing against me, I could feel the sounds through his body as well.

"Is this what you wanted to show me?" I asked.

Ethan didn't look at me this time, turning back to the track. "I used to come here often when I was younger. We'd talk about engines and specs and which teams would win. And when I wanted to be alone, I'd let the roar of the engines drown out my thoughts."

I studied his face as he mused about his past. He was not quite the same boy I'd remembered from the woods, nor the dashing playboy I'd met at the Conservation Fund event. This Ethan was an entirely different entity. Serious, pensive, philosophical. Was this the real Ethan or just another one of his many faces? In that moment, it didn't feel like it mattered much. What mattered to me was that he'd shared this with me.

I tiptoed up and kissed him lightly on the lips.

Somehow that felt appropriate.

Then we both turned back to the track, standing side by side, watching the colors blur past us, letting the afternoon float away.

Very Important People

"Mr. Thorne! Mr. Thorne!"

Ethan and I both turned our heads to see a short man dressed in a simple black suit waving frantically at us. I was surprised that we could even hear his voice over the track. He rushed over to us, hopping over a low barrier. I turned to Ethan, who wore a deepening frown.

Ethan quickly slid his lanyard off and I followed suit. He took the fake badge from me and tucked both pieces of evidence into his pocket. His frown seemed to be stamped on his face.

This must have been the reason why we had to be particularly sneaky and careful. Images of being escorted out by security flashed through my mind as I tried not to panic.

Ethan stepped in front of me as the short hurried man reached us.

"It's always a pleasure to have you with us, sir," the man said, dusting himself off and placing his hands together primly.

"Hello Tristan," Ethan said, placing an arm around my back, motioning toward the door. "We were just about to leave."

"Oh no no no!" Tristan grasped Ethan's hand with both of his own and shook it with much gusto. "You can't possibly. I'm terribly sorry that you weren't greeted at the gate, we had no idea you were coming. Those interns in the office must've forgotten to write it down on the schedule, you see. The thing is, the management office always hires recent college graduates and the young ones these days don't know the difference between a hard day's work and their bungholes. Again, you must accept our deepest apologies."

Tristan was apologizing so profusely that sweat was beginning to bead on his brow even though he'd probably just stepped outside. A rivulet of sweat ran into his eye which made him stop talking for a moment. He produced a white handkerchief from his suit pocket and dabbed away the sweat before continuing. "Thank the Lord that I spotted you on the cameras. It's so terribly hot out here. Simply appalling that you were made to get lost...and with a guest no less!"

I snuck a glance at Ethan and we shared a smile as the man continued talking. I was beginning to wonder if Tristan was the reason that we'd had to get staff passes and sneak in.

Tristan continued rambling, "...and the entire bar has just been remodeled in an art nouveau style by a French interior designer — you absolutely must see the stamped tin ceilings — oh and our new chef was personally trained in Vienna by Hans Hirschl himself who developed the menu and — look at me getting ahead of myself. You'll see it all for yourself soon enough. You must be dying in this heat what with the..."

Ethan's eyes glazed over as he waited for Tristan to finish. Finally he turned to me and asked, "Would you like to see the sky box?"

"I suppose a girl could be convinced," I said coyly.

"Good, it'll be easier this way," he said.

I was a little confused about why Ethan didn't seem too excited. I'd only seen so many VIP spaces as an event runner as well as a flower courier, but to actually get to enjoy one of those spaces seemed like a thrilling opportunity, even if Tristan was a bit overwhelming.

"Excellent!" Tristan swiftly chirped. "You simply must allow me to escort you there."

The short man hopped spryly to the door and opened it for us, waving us through graciously. As I stepped through, I heard Tristan mumbling into his staff's earpiece that *the* Mr. Ethan Thorne was on his way to the sky box.

A short elevator ride later and we were at the top of the stadium in a quiet hallway, far above the noise and smells and chaos on the track.

I noticed that the floors here were of tiled marble, elegant and refined, unlike the plain concrete of the lower levels.

Tristan led us to the door at the end of the hallway and ushered us inside.

We found ourselves in a massive lounge area, replete with dark leather couches. On one end of the large, open room was a fully stocked bar with a bartender. On the other end was a set of tables with a massive spread of food including lobster tails, caviar tins on ice, and plates of multi-colored hor d'oeuvres.

But what drew my attention the most was the floor to ceiling windows directly across from us. They were so large that we could see the entire crowd seated in the stadium opposite us and the full track beneath us, the race cars like little toys from this height, zipping along the track. And to ensure that no detail of the race would be missed, there were TV screens mounted along the walls to give us a track level view of the race.

I let a small gasp escape from my lips.

"Much more comfortable, yes?" Tristan's smile brightened, and then he turned to Ethan. "Please enjoy yourself Mr. Thorne. And if there is anything, and I mean *anything*, that you or your guest require, please let a member of the staff know and we shall arrange it for you."

Tristan took his leave while Ethan was still looking around the room, preoccupied.

He seemed rather tense, uneasy. Though I could see no reason to be. Sharing the lounge with us were only five other guests, drinks in hand, their backs to us, watching the race. Given that Ethan had spoken to a far larger crowd at the Conservation Fund, I couldn't imagine that he was uncomfortable with socializing.

Ethan placed a hand on my elbow and guided me to the far end of the lounge, away from the other guests in the room, but we were interrupted after a few steps.

"If it isn't Ethan Thorne!" A very loud, very Southern, bellowing voice declared.

We both turned to see a heavy-set mustached man in a tan suit, bolo tie, a thick leather belt with an oversized buckle, walking over to us. The only item missing was a cowboy hat, which I noticed the attractive woman standing next to him was holding delicately in her manicured hands.

Ethan slipped his hand off my elbow and his face shifted into a calm, pleasant smile so quickly that it was uncanny.

"You got me, guilty as charged." He chuckled and thrust his hand out toward the man. "My memory escapes me, but I believe we met at the Met Gala... Dale Sutton's brother if I'm not mistaken?"

The large man accepted Ethan's hand and pumped it up and down, up and down, his face turning even redder. "Why yes! Name's George," he said, slurring slightly. It was barely one in the afternoon, but I suppose given the festive atmosphere it made sense that the drinks were flowing.

"This here's my old lady, Michelle," he said, motioning to his wife who stepped forward and offered her free hand to Ethan with a limp wrist. The woman was wearing a shimmery dress of colorful sequins, which hugged her curves. She seemed at least twenty years younger than him—hardly an "old lady."

"What a pleasure to meet you, *Ethan*," the woman sang with her southern twang. Her eyelashes fluttered and if I didn't know better, I'd say she was trying to openly use a 'come hither' look on Ethan.

Ethan merely tilted his head pleasantly, and brought her hand close to his face before releasing it.

George cut in, "Say Ethan, what'dya figure's gonna happen with the crude futures with everything those A-rabs are doing?"

His wife pouted then turned to me, eyes flashing excitedly. "Let's you and I head on over and leave the men to their boring chatter, shall we? Ethan, be a doll and introduce us, would you?"

Ethan slid his arm around my waist. "Sierra and I were just stopping by, we'll have to be on our way shortly."

Following Ethan's lead, I smiled awkwardly, unsure of what was expected of me. It was all a little overwhelming, and I was starting to see why Ethan had been hesitant about coming here.

"Oh no, that's too soon!" George bellowed. "You haven't even let the lady have a drink yet!"

Michelle sidled over and mock whispered, "I'd skip the drinks if I were you. The help here can't be bothered to learn how to make a proper Manhattan, or any other drink for that matter."

It seemed a bit rude to complain that loudly about the drinks, especially since it seemed like her husband had enjoyed quite a few of them already, but I just smiled pleasantly and nodded.

Somehow, George had already managed to engage Ethan in conversation through sheer persistence and suddenly I found myself alone with Michelle.

She flashed a fake smile at me, shaking her head disappointedly at the conversation happening next to us. "So, who are you wearing?"

"Who am I...what?"

She flourished her hand down the front of her dress, presenting it to me, "Lagerfeld. It's his latest line. I managed to snatch it up before it debuts in Milan next season."

I made a show of admiring her dress, noting that the sequins formed a wave-like pattern. April would call it a statement dress, but I had a feeling this woman dressed in statement dresses all the time.

"It's very nice," I said, finally.

"Thank you," she said in a way that made it seem like she'd expecting a bigger reaction. "It's so much work these days to keep up with what's in season so most women don't even bother to put in the effort."

I couldn't tell if we were talking about fashion or produce anymore, but either way, Michelle's snooty attitude was more than a little off-putting so I just nodded politely without adding anything to the conversation.

Unfortunately, it seemed that Michelle didn't need my input before she started prattling off a long list of designers and explaining the pros and cons of the fashion trends this year, leaning more opinionated than informative. I managed to paste a smile on my face and nod at the appropriate moments.

Finally, Ethan turned to me, grabbed my arm and loudly interrupted, "Sierra, we can't be late for the…"

"Of course," I said, reacting quickly. "Please excuse us, Michelle, we have to head over to the uh… It was wonderful chatting with you,"

Ethan and I took the opening to make our exit, walking quickly to the elevator without a word. When the doors finally closed, I let out a loud sigh.

"Did you know that was going to happen?" I asked Ethan.

He shrugged, "The cast changes, but the show remains the same."

"Well, I suppose I've gotten my fill of VIP rooms then," I said, laughing. "So where to next? We've seen the skybox, we've been track level. I suppose the only thing left is the concession stand?"

"As a matter of fact, there is one last place we haven't been yet," Ethan said, a luring smile forming on his face as he removed the staff passes from his pocket and dangled them in front of me.

I wasn't sure where Ethan was taking me, but the more I learned about him, the more comfortable I felt around him. In the VIP box, though he was clearly very practiced in interacting with the charming Suttons, he hadn't wanted to schmooze with them any longer than I had.

I'd had plenty of unpleasant experiences dealing with people like Mr. and Mrs. Sutton, having worked a number of high end events, but somehow I imagined that Ethan would fit right in with them. I was happy to be proven wrong.

Perhaps it shouldn't have come as such a surprise to me that Ethan wouldn't enjoy spending so much time around the VIP crowd, but it was still welcome.

Ethan and I shared light banter as we made our way to the outer rim of the Speedway complex. The place was massive, but luckily, Ethan had found a golf cart that the staff used for traveling between buildings which I was rather grateful for, having tired myself out from all the walking already.

Finally, we found ourselves in front of a flat building with a row of pristine garage doors, each numbered, but with no signage otherwise.

Ethan parked the golf cart out front and beeped us into the building with his staff pass, while I tried to ignore the large number of security cameras pointed at us.

Unlike the outside, the inside was a bustling city. Engineers dressed in coveralls were rushing back and forth everywhere. In the station closest to us, a Formula one car was hoisted on a hydraulic lift, with a crew of five engineers working on various parts.

Though nearly every station was full, no one paid us any attention, despite the fact that even if we were "staff," we were definitely not the right kind of staff to belong in here.

Ethan walked smoothly, knowing exactly where we were headed, until we reached a station where a lanky, thickly bearded engineer in neon green coveralls was banging around under the hood of what appeared to be a fancy sports car.

The engineer jerked upright, nearly hitting his head, looked at me—his eyes wide behind his safety goggles—looked at Ethan, then looked at me again. He had a mass of long blonde hair that fell down to his shoulders.

"Jesus, Mary and Joseph, who died?" he said in a thick Aussie accent, a disbelieving grin spreading across his face. He wiped his grease covered hands on his coveralls before walking over to Ethan and embracing him in a giant bear hug. "It's been a long time, my man."

Ethan returned the hug, slapping the man heartily on the back.

"What can I say," Ethan shrugged, smiling wider than I'd ever seen him smile, "things have been crazy."

"No shit eh?" the engineer said, then turned his attention to me, elbowing Ethan comically, a teasing look on his face.

"Sierra, this is Jackson, we went to college together," Ethan said, "Jackson, this is Sierra, we —"

"No need to explain," Jackson cut in, grinning cheekily at me as he offered his hand.

I laughed, shaking Jackson's hand. Something about his directness was very refreshing, especially after that awful interaction with Mr. and Mrs. Sutton in the VIP Box. "Very nice to meet you Jackson."

Jackson stuck two fingers into his mouth and let out a piercing whistle. All activity around us simply stopped, every engineer freezing at their stations, tools still in hand, turning to Jackson, and by extension, Ethan and I.

Jackson put his arm around Ethan's shoulder and turned to the engineers watching us, a big smile on his face. "Oy, listen here! My good mate Ethan has descended from his perch atop his boardroom to grace us with a visit today...with a *lady* friend!"

This induced a round of hollering and whistling from the engineers.

"You all know what that means...let's break early, you greasy cunts!"

Another chorus of cheers rose up as tools were dropped right at their stations and nearly a hundred oil rags came out as all the engineers wiped their hands simultaneously.

"I hope we're not disrupting anything," Ethan said.

Jackson shook his head, "We're not the pit mechanics, so we've got nothing to do with *that* race. And hey, see this?" he underlined the nameplate on his breast pocket which had his name and "Director of R&D" embossed in shiny brass, "I got promoted! And you know what that means. Now I'm the *director* of racing and dicking around!"

Jackson turned to me, gave me a wink, and covered the side of his mouth as if he were whispering. "Just ask Ethan, back in the day, he was the worst offender."

I tried to picture a younger Ethan working here, slipping away to the main track to listen to the roar of the cars. Was this where he'd developed his love for engineering or had that come earlier?

"Is that so?" I asked, in pretend shock. "Ethan Thorne, breaking the rules? Slacking off at work? I can't possibly imagine it."

Ethan shrugged, but didn't deny it. "We did have our fun."

"Come on then," Jackson said, waving us over to the exit door at the back of the building, "enough dicking around, it's time to race!"

I wasn't exactly sure what he meant by "race," but that quickly became clear after we followed him outside to the sunny lot behind the building.

An intricate yet unpolished mini-track had been set up on the asphalt, complete with stacks of tires lining the corners, and red-and-white plastic barriers bordering the sides. Most of the engineers were already out there, hooting loudly as they watched their buddies zoom around the track in go-karts.

"Ethan here used to be a crack driver," Jackson said. "He ever tell you that?"

I thought back to our drive in the rental Camry and didn't remember any fancy moves he'd pulled, but then again, after that moment on the main race-track, it didn't surprise me at all. It seemed that I was learning all sorts of secrets from Jackson today.

"Did he used to win a lot of your races?" I asked.

"You bet! Although, I don't recall him ever racing a lady…" Jackson tapped his chin in thought, then added, "And you're the first lady he's brought to meet old Jackson so perhaps we'll see an end to Ethan's reign yet?"

Hearing the roar of the engines at the main track had gotten my blood pumping and a lap around their miniature track here seemed like the perfect way to have a little fun.

I punched Ethan playfully on the arm, "So? How about it? Think you can put your skills to the test?"

Ethan shook his head. "We are definitely not racing. There aren't even any safety regulations on this track."

That was rich coming from Ethan. I looked over at Jackson who clearly shared my sentiment.

"What's life without a little danger?" I said, puffing out my chest like a macho caricature of how I pictured a younger Ethan.

"She stole your line there, mate," Jackson said, slapping his leg in laughter.

Ethan shook his head and sighed, knowing that he'd already lost the fight. "I can take you around the track for a couple of laps, but absolutely no racing."

I put a finger on his chest, "I'll have you know I've been driving the van for my shop for years, and if I can handle L.A. traffic, I can handle driving on a closed track."

"These aren't your amusement park go karts," Ethan said. "And as much as I trust Jackson's engineering skills, they weren't designed for safety nor a smooth ride."

"We've made a few *minor* adjustments," Jackson agreed, holding his thumb and forefinger together.

I looked over at the track again. Tires squealed loudly as the engineers caromed around the turns, filling the air with the smell of burnt rubber. As they zipped by, I noticed that no two karts looked exactly alike. Each one had different engine attachments jerry-rigged on, with various aerodynamic features fastened to the frames that looked like they were salvaged from the scrap pile.

I didn't remember ever seeing go karts that fast, and now, looking at those dubiously constructed open frames, Ethan's warnings about safety regulations didn't seem all that unreasonable.

Still, if this was how Ethan liked to have his fun when he was younger, I wasn't willing to let the opportunity slide without at least experiencing it for myself.

"Fine, no racing," I conceded, "but I'm driving my own kart."

Definitely Not Racing

A few minutes later, I found myself sitting in the cockpit of one of the heavily modified go karts with a helmet on my head, staring down at the stretch of track before me, wondering just what the hell I'd gotten myself into.

Once the engine rumbled to life, it was clear that these were a far cry from the go karts at the local county fair. The vibrations buzzing from the hard plastic seat beneath me had my teeth chattering so hard I was afraid I might chip a tooth.

And I hadn't even started driving.

Well, it was far too late to back out now. I'd talked myself into this. I looked over at Ethan, seeing only the reflection from his helmet visor of myself and gave him a thumbs up.

He gave me a thumbs up back.

On the side of the track, Jackson held his arm up and dramatically slashed it down. Even though we'd agreed that we weren't racing, I suppose it was ceremonial.

Ethan took off, his cart heading down the track. I guess he forgot that we weren't supposed to be racing. Maybe seeing Jackson give the starting cue had triggered some instinctive response in him.

I wasn't about to let that go unchallenged, so I floored the gas.

The engine rumbled even louder and I braced my back against the seat, gripping the steering wheel tighter, preparing to slingshot down the track.

But the kart didn't move. Instead, it sat there in the middle of the asphalt like a lump of cement.

What the hell?

I pumped the gas pedal.

This time, a weak sputtering sound came from the engine.

When I craned my neck around, I saw a puff of black smoke escape.

Well, that didn't seem good.

Ethan came back around, finishing his lap quickly. He pulled over next to me and climbed out of his kart, taking his helmet off as he walked over.

"What seems to be the problem?" he asked, crouching down next to me.

I removed my helmet as well so that I could see better.

"I don't know," I said, shrugging, "seems a little bit *suspicious*, like *someone* could have sabotaged my kart because they were afraid of me winning..." I wagged my finger at Ethan playfully.

Ethan just laughed. "Let me take a look."

Without missing a beat, he bent down in front of the kart, poking around the gear shift between my legs.

"Careful there! Are you sure you know what you're doing?" I asked, a bit of concern and amusement in my voice.

Ethan gave me a wink. "Don't worry, I'm certified." Then he turned over his shoulder, calling out to Jackson, "Can I get a three quarter wrench here?"

Jackson jogged out onto the track and handed one to Ethan. "You need me to have a look at that?"

"I might be spending more time in the boardroom these days, but even I can spot a dirty carburetor."

Ethan took the wrench from Jackson and worked on a bolt. Seeing the muscles of his forearm tense as he worked between my legs was giving me all sorts of ideas that had nothing to do with engines. I licked my lips and watched Ethan to see if he was thinking the same thing, but his eyes were intent, focused on the problem at hand. Boy, a focused man could be so terribly seductive.

After letting some liquid drain out, Ethan tightened the bolt back up again, and patted me on the thigh.

"Try it now," he said.

I stepped on the gas pedal, and this time the engine rumbled into action. Ethan shot me a smile, then headed back to his kart. It didn't take too much imagination to see a younger Ethan spending his days here, working on these engines and racing around with his buddies. April probably would have said that the kart breaking down was the universe's way of letting me see that side of Ethan.

Jackson got back into his position by the starting line, gave us another countdown and slashed his arm again.

This time, when I floored the gas, the kart rocketed down the tiny track.

The rest of the drive was an adrenaline pumping blur.

The turns came at me so fast that I didn't have time to analyze them or fill myself with anxiety and dread; all I could do was react. And react I did, driving the best I had ever driven. Then again, I didn't recall ever driving the flower van this aggressively. I always planned ahead to ensure that I wouldn't have to take on the L.A. highways like a psychopath.

Of course, it didn't take long for Ethan to catch up with me, and we traded positions for a bit, not being too gentle with each other as we bumped and slid past each other. There were a few passes that I felt Ethan could have taken but was too polite to, but other than that, I could tell he was having a good time, and so was I.

Then, in a flash, the "race" was over, and I crossed the finish line, Ethan right on my rear. I pulled over to the side and clambered out, my heart still pounding in my chest, adrenaline making my hands shaky, my legs wobbly.

I couldn't remember the last time I had so much fun, and I was grateful that Ethan had driven hard, even if I was pretty sure he'd taken it easy on me.

Ethan slipped out of his kart with experienced grace. His hair was damp and messy, his hands were still greasy from fixing my kart and there was a slight flush to his cheeks, like one might expect from another heart pounding activity. Was that how he looked after sex? There was an insistent urging in my chest to find out, especially after I'd seen him working between my legs earlier.

I walked over to Ethan and kissed him, not even caring that we were in public. Ethan pulled me in closer, his lips slightly salty, his face smelling slightly of motor oil and sun, and we stayed like that for some time.

When we broke apart, the rest of the world returned to my senses and I realized that Jackson and the other engineers were cheering uproariously, as if they were celebrating the winner of the Monaco Grand Prix.

"What was that for?" Ethan murmured, his eyes twinkling.

"Your consolation prize," I said, my heart soaring. "With more to come."

What We Deserve

The bedroom of Ethan's suite at the Imperial Grand Hotel was furnished with a cushioned fabric headboard above the extravagant king-sized bed, the walls holding mirrors framed in ornate silver, but all I could think about was the pounding in my chest.

We'd returned once more to the scene of the crime, where we'd both made mistakes. If rooms held memories of its occupants, I wondered if our mistakes were permanently stored within these walls.

If they were, what chance did we stand of correcting the past?

I brushed a strand of hair away from my forehead, still slightly damp from the heat outside.

Ethan watched me, not saying a word.

We'd joked and teased each other the entire drive back, but now that we'd found ourselves in his bedroom, we were both suddenly short on words. The world outside was full of noise and bustle but the cool darkness of the bedroom was silent, sacred.

"Would you like another one of those?" Ethan asked, his voice husky. He pointed to the Chianti in my hand.

I shook my head.

"I'm fully capable of making my mistakes while sober," I joked.

Ethan chuckled, nodding.

"We don't have to do this," Ethan said, even as he stepped closer to me, his eyes hungry, roaming over my skin.

Yes, we did, I thought.

His chest rose and fell slowly, the hint of his nipples under the fabric. I watched the condensation on his wine glass, beading, then growing, then slowly making trails down the glass. I watched his fingers, curling around the stem of his wine glass, powerful and firm, like he could snap the slender glass in a moment if he chose to, and I remembered when those same fingers were wrapped around a Martini glass, not so long ago.

We stood in front of each other, the space between us crackling, like an invisible barrier built from everything we'd left unspoken.

We'd already been over the formalities the last time we'd been in his suite, though we hadn't managed to make it all the way to the bedroom. This time, we could breeze past them without slowing down. The contracts had already been signed and sealed, all that remained was the final pen stroke.

I finished the rest of my Chianti in one long gulp, and set my wine glass down, on the edge of the night stand.

Ethan mirrored me, placing his glass next to mine.

I didn't need to touch him to know that he was tense. Underneath his blue polo his muscles were coiled, holding something back. But tonight, we didn't need to hold back. We'd held back enough already, we'd held back enough to last us a lifetime.

That night after the Conservation Fund, my reasons for having sex with Ethan were all wrong, twisted by my shock at seeing him again, distorted by my denial of my true feelings.

Tonight would be different.

Ethan had shown me a lot about him these past few days, letting me see him for who he was, inviting me into his world. It felt only right to for me to take the final step here, in the bedroom, especially with what had happened the first time we'd ended up here.

Fingers trembling, I unbuttoned my blouse, feeling the smooth fabric pull and then release around each plastic pebble.

The blouse fell to the floor.

A shock of cold air hit me from the vent above, making goosebumps rise all over my naked skin. A shiver ran up my spine and I felt a strong urge to cover up my cleavage, this sudden shyness and insecurity coming out of nowhere, but I resisted the urge to hide, letting my arms hang at my sides instead.

We'd done enough hiding.

Ethan's eyes roamed over me, drinking me in, consuming me. An intense fire was burning behind those dark eyes as they caught for a moment at my cleavage, then slid over my white, lacey bra.

"Are you sure about this?" he asked, his brows furrowed.

The question felt out of character for the Ethan I'd known as a child. The younger Ethan never worried about my doubts. That Ethan always knew, assumed, I could take it. Back then, all that was at stake were scraped knees and poison ivy rashes, but now we were older. More fragile.

I nodded, but didn't make eye contact. Instead, I let my own eyes fully take in the sight of Ethan. The cotton shirt covering his skin still contained his mysteries, but once he took it off, we'd both be bare in front of one another.

Ethan's forearms tensed, and in one smooth motion he tore his shirt off over his head, setting it down beside him.

My breath caught. I couldn't help myself as I gazed over his chiseled body. The smooth round nipples—dark against his broad chest, the shadows and valleys of his abs, the ripples of his rib cage as they rose and fell heavily.

His skin looked like burnished oak in the soft yellow light and I wondered how it would feel under my fingers. How it would taste. Would it be hot to the touch? Or cool?

Without taking our eyes off of each other, we undressed ourselves, stepping out of our shoes, our pants—Ethan pulling off his belt with a soft thwhipping sound—not rushing, yet not stalling either, until we were both down to our underwear.

Ethan wore a pair of black, silky boxer-briefs. His thighs strained against the tight fabric, as if they could burst forth at any moment, and my eyes caught on his package, round and powerful.

There was no need for pretense in this space.

I knew what I wanted. If I was being honest with myself, I'd already known what I wanted that night our eyes first met at the Conservation Fund event, but I'd been too afraid to accept it at the time. I was ready to throw it all away for one night of heated passion. But Ethan had put a stop to that. He'd known who I was and had seen through my ruse.

Now, I was grateful that he had.

Ethan's shoulders were rising and falling, practically heaving.

"We can stop at any time, Sierra," he said, his voice squeezing shut toward the end like he wasn't sure he'd be able to stop any time, like it was foolish to even suggest such a thing.

In which case he'd be right.

We couldn't. No more stopping. No more waiting.

I removed my bra, letting it fall to the floor, and slipped my underwear off, stepping out of them, before I could stop myself.

My cheeks flushed with heat from how vulnerable I felt, standing there naked in front of Ethan, feeling his eyes take in my breasts, my cleft. Need coiled somewhere deep in my abdomen, and I realized suddenly that I couldn't wait any longer.

If the last few bars of this song needed to be rushed, then that was far preferable to the alternative. I stepped over to him, and trembling, pressed my palm against the outside of his boxer-briefs.

Heat. Pure heat radiated through the fabric and into my skin. Then I felt his cock straining, eager and hard against my hand.

Ethan tensed at my touch.

I leaned against his chest, placing my ear against his ribcage, listening, letting my own pounding pulse slow and match his heartbeat, strong and insistent, my breasts brushing against his skin.

"I've never done this before," Ethan said.

The thought of Ethan Thorne as a virgin was so ridiculous that I giggled, though that may have been more from nerves than anything else.

"You're not a good liar," I whispered, leaving a kiss on his broad flat chest, inhaling his deep masculine scent. Ethan's skin smelled of old mahogany and polished leather, with a faint undertone of clean sea salt. I could feel myself getting a little dizzy.

I reached into his underwear, my fingers pushing back the elastic band, until I found what I wanted, rolling it in my palm. His cock felt thick and weighty in my hands, the skin like burning velvet.

Ethan groaned, throwing his head back, closing his eyes.

"This is different," he growled, the words coming from somewhere low in his belly.

"I know what you mean," I said, pulling his underwear to the floor, freeing him.

We couldn't be each other's firsts, that opportunity lost to us through time, but that didn't mean it wouldn't be memorable, making its mark in both of our timelines.

Ethan's chest rose and fell, his arms tensing.

He pressed into me, embracing me in his powerful arms, enrobing me in a kiss. His cock was hard and hot against my belly, burning my skin like a brand. Our lips crashed together, our tongues desperately exploring, yearning for contact. We fought for a moment, until Ethan overcame me, claiming my mouth as he devoured my lips.

We broke apart, but just for an instant, before his lips were on my neck, kissing, sucking, nibbling their way down to the hollow of my shoulder.

"I want every piece of you," he whispered into my neck.

I could only moan as I yielded to him, letting him pick me up and carry me like I was just a doll, laying me on top of the crisp, cold sheets of the bed.

Slowly, painstakingly, Ethan kissed my body, building the heat within me. He started from the tops of my feet, made his way up my calves, lingering longer at where my thighs met my body, then continuing onward to the ticklish skin around my belly button.

When he reached my nipples, I gasped at the wet warm heat of his mouth. He took my nipples into his mouth, rolling them delicately between his lips, licking and suckling, sending shivers of pleasure up and down my spine, until all I could think about was more. More pleasure. More Ethan.

He towered over me then, and my body knew what to do. My legs spread open against his powerful thighs, the void in my sex aching to be filled.

He prepared himself.

Then our eyes met and held the connection as he pressed his cock against my need. Arching into him, I yearned for more, for him to finally be inside of me, for him to take me and release the tension that I'd held onto for so long.

"You're so wet," he said, teasing the head of his cock against my entrance.

And then he slid into my pussy, making me yield and stretch and take him.

The pleasure was so intense it made my knees shake, so I clamped them around his sides, pulling him deeper.

We continued in that position, riding each other, holding on so desperately that we couldn't tell where one began and the other ended, panting and moaning and kissing.

Until finally the pleasure was far too much to bear and it seemed like the room exploded in lights. I came, and faintly, I could feel Ethan coming soon after, my pussy clenching around his throbbing cock.

Waves of emotion washed through me, cracking something that had been inside me for almost as long as I could remember. The world around me faded into a blissful haze.

When I came back, I realized I was crying.

How could he… How could *I* deserve all of this? How could I deserve the man, who was so sweet and caring, that had grown up from the boy that I'd wounded so badly?

Tears flowed freely down my face, as I clutched Ethan's shoulders, releasing long wracking sobs into his chest. My tears had mixed with his sweat, making his skin damp and slippery.

From far away, I could hear Ethan trying to say something to me.

I wiped my watery eyes to see him better. Ethan was looking at me, his face concerned.

"Did I hurt you?" he asked, eyes wide.

The question made me want to cry even more, but I bit my trembling lip down. Ethan was so concerned about me, so worried about hurting me, when I'd never even apologized for hurting him all those years ago. But I tried to control my breathing, finally calming down.

"No Ethan, not at all," I said, barely a whisper. I knew he could never hurt me like that.

He nodded, but didn't seem convinced. Instead he rolled onto his back on the other side of the bed.

Exhausted from everything that had happened that day, I struggled to keep my eyes open. The last thing I remembered before drifting off was Ethan's face beside me, his brow furrowed.

The Little Things

"How'd it go?" I asked April as she bounded out from the back door of La Vernisage, a popular event spot we'd delivered to countless times. I'd driven us there and stayed with the van—at April's insistence. Since she was going to be out the rest of the week, she had volunteered to do the dropoff for this particular wedding.

April rolled her eyes. "The mother of the bride insisted on picking out the biggest roses and swapping them into the bouquets for her own table."

"Yikes," I said.

"But after that, it went fine. Thanks for letting me take the rest of the week off," she said.

"Of course, girl," I said. "You can't get roles if you don't do auditions."

I grinned and got in the van cheerfully, though internally I was wondering how I'd be able to make it through an entire week alone in the shop without April to keep me company.

This week hadn't come entirely as a surprise, April had been booking more and more gigs and with her filming for this new indie project and some intensive final round auditions for a big hush hush studio film. I knew she'd be busy, I only wish that I'd planned ahead. Even Ethan wouldn't serve as a good distraction, since he'd told me that he would need to return to San Francisco for some business, and that he'd be in touch.

April buckled up and we headed off back to the shop.

"So," April started, with a coy tone, "When's it going to happen for you and Ethan?"

"When's what going to happen?" I asked, genuinely confused.

"You know, walk down the aisle, big bash, all the celebs there, Ryan Gosling spots me and just *loves* my dress…"

I laughed. It'd been a while since I talked to April about Ethan, and she hadn't gotten into the usual barrage of questions either. I figured it was because she'd been busy with her auditions, but apparently she hadn't forgotten entirely.

"Well," I started, "you're going to need to back it up for me and explain how you got to Ethan and I getting hitched."

April tapped her chin. "Okay, so let me see. Ethan acted like a total jerk the first night you met him, and you told me all about it. Then he came to the flower shop, acting like a presumptuous ass, and you told me all about it. *Then* you go on a few dates with him and suddenly you're *suspiciously* mum, *ergo*...you two must be getting ready for the honeymoon."

"Wow," I said, "That is...um...quite a stretch. Besides, I *did* tell you about our date! You scared the crap out of me by hiding in the shadows of my apartment. Don't tell me you forgot about that. A certain someone said they pee—"

April cleared her throat so loudly I thought she might choke up a frog. "Your exact words were: 'It was nice,' with a *dreamy* look in your eyes."

"Okay, I did not have a dreamy look in my eyes, let's get that straight. And I didn't mean to shut you out but we've barely had a chance to talk at all this past week," I protested.

April looked at the GPS on my phone. "We've got thirty-five whole minutes. You better dish, girl."

I sighed, but was kind of grateful that even with April's hectic life she still cared enough to nag me about Ethan. To be honest, I'd been wanting to talk to her about what had happened anyway, especially given the newer, more *physical* developments. So for the rest of the drive I filled her in on the details of our first date and our more recent expedition to the race track, and April just about had a heart attacked over Ethan fixing my go-kart.

I tried to only hint at what had happened between Ethan and I afterwards, but April managed to pry most of it out of me anyway. I was just grateful she didn't need the play by play, she was content to accept my blushing cheeks as answer enough.

"That sounds really great, I'm so happy for you," she said after I'd finished, hugging me, even though I was still driving.

"Thanks," I said. After a moment, I added, "But...it's just that sometimes I get this paranoid feeling that it's all going to come crashing down at any moment."

April frowned. "Why do you say that?"

"Well, he's gone for business this entire week and his company's in San Francisco and I don't know how it's going to work with us being in different towns and..."

Would we technically be considered long distance even though we were in the same state? Don't long distance relationships always end in disaster? I felt like I'd read that in a blog somewhere. A thousand other concerns jumbled together in my mind, all trying to get out, until I just gave up and sighed.

"Maybe I'm just some L.A. booty call."

April's jaw practically dropped to the floor. "Are you joking?"

"Maybe he has some other flower shop girl in S.F."

"Oh sure, another someone he's known since he was a child." I could almost see the sarcasm dripping from her mouth as she rolled her eyes. "Come on, Sierra."

I frowned at her, pouting a bit. I must have looked pretty close to the petulant child I felt like I was.

April sighed heavily, then straightened her back, placing her hands firmly on her small hips. "Have you been keeping in touch?"

"We're just texting back and forth and —"

"Nev," April cut in.

"What?"

"It sounds like everything's going great."

I managed to mumble some half-hearted gibberish.

"Listen to me Nev," she went in for her signature April hug, "everything is *okay*."

"I know," I said, though it wasn't very convincing, even to myself.

April sighed and pulled away, placing her warm hand on my shoulder. "You're a hotshot female entrepreneur, Ethan's landing multi-billion dollar contracts and modeling for the cover of Forbes, I'm sure you can figure out how to travel between San Francisco and Los Angeles between the two of you."

I was quiet, trying to let April's words comfort me. Deep down I knew she was right, but some irrational, terrified part of me had trouble accepting it.

"Just let yourself enjoy it girl!" April continued, instantly discerning the worry in my face. "Don't sabotage yourself just because you're not in control of exactly how everything is going to play out. If you guys love each other, the little things will work themselves out."

"The little things could also eat us alive."

"Only if you dwell on them, and obsess over them."

I nodded, trying to take April's words to heart, but the only thing I could focus on was the one question that she'd inadvertently raised. How little did those "little things" have to be in order to work themselves out?

Donut Girl

I opened the heavy metal door, sliding a wooden wedge under it to keep it open, and greeted Niko.

The guy was barely smiling, the epitome of the cool, silent type, and was standing outside in the alley. "You have delivery, yes?"

"I sure do," I said cheerily, taking the invoice that he offered me.

As I checked it over, Niko craned his neck to look inside the store. "Where is donut girl today?"

I smiled inwardly. Boy was April going to hear about this. The new delivery guy she'd been swooning over could very well be swooning back.

"April's off today, but she'll be back next week. Should we get to unloading?"

After moving all the boxes into the shop, sending Niko on his way, and then preparing the flowers, I stared glumly at the clock.

Barely noon and I'd already eaten my lunch. This day was dragging on forever. Normally the days seemed to fly by, but I couldn't understand why today felt so long.

I strung up the cardboard boxes from the delivery into a tight bundle.

How would I tell April about Niko?

I grinned, then breezed through some possible clever opens:

Guess who asked for you at the shop?

Have you been daydreaming about anyone with tattoos lately?

Have you always wanted to have someone endearingly nickname you donut girl?

I tried not to laugh out loud to myself at that last one.

With April running to auditions all week, I had the shop all to myself. Normally, work was distracting enough, but today, it just wasn't cutting it. On weekdays like today, there usually weren't a lot of walk-ins, but I'd gotten used to it by now. It wasn't my favorite part about running the shop, since the big money was always in the events and holidays, but it did keep the lights on.

I stared at the bell on our front door, but even if I shot lasers out of my eyes, it wouldn't ring, signalling a new customer, distracting me and whisking me away into any sort of interesting situation, even if it was another lizard lady. At least a lizard lady would add some umph to the day.

Man, was I losing it, or what?

I decided to sweep up.

On the first round, I swept away all of the scattered leaf clippings on the floor behind the counter. Since it was an area that customers never saw, we'd gotten a little lax on maintenance. After that, I dusted off all the vases on the shelves, and rearranged the window display. I even took the trouble to take multiple trips outside to get an idea of what a passersby on the street might notice.

All of that work barely took an hour.

I tapped my chin and looked around the shop, searching for something else to do. My eyes landed on the wall of multi-colored ribbons. The last time they'd been organized by color had been when we first opened the shop.

April had an annoying habit of hanging the spools back on the wall haphazardly, which left it looking like a clown's coat. April's method resulted in more popularly requested colors naturally grouping to the easy-to-reach locations, but other more unique colors ended up scattered and hidden, making them ridiculously time consuming to find. No amount of badgering her about it had ever helped and all my protests about how it'd be easier to find all the colors if they were properly organized had fallen on deaf ears.

It'd be a pretty monumental task.

The perfect distraction for the rest of the day!

I located some small empty clear plastic bins to help with the process when my eyes couldn't help but land on the crimson colored spool.

After Ethan's first impromptu visit to the shop, he never mentioned it again, but I hadn't forgotten about it, tucked away in my nightstand as I slept.

I thought vaguely on the advice April had given me and had let her meaning sink in over the next few days. I had to admit that I was feeling better about it, allowing myself to take it easy and not get all up in my head about how our relationship was progressing. The intense emotions that Ethan had bubbled in me from our physical relationship were still there, but I was getting a better handle on managing them and treating it like the light-hearted fun that it was.

Still, I couldn't help but feel a sense of restlessness.

I took out my phone and tapped out a quick message to Ethan. Maybe he'd be in a mood to chat, or at least get back to me by the time I finished organizing the ribbons.

How's work? Boring here at the shop today.

I sent off the message and got started on the ribbons.

The reorganization turned out to be far less work than I'd hoped, and I had it all done in half an hour. It's wild the amount of work you can get done when you get in the zone and carried away. Before I could admire my handiwork, I'd noticed that Ethan had gotten back to my message.

Same old. I'll talk to you soon.

It seemed like Ethan was too busy for a chat, and I didn't want to bother him more so I just left it at that.

I sighed, then took a moment to appreciate the ribbon wall. It hadn't been as distracting as I thought it would be, but at least the wall finally looked the way it should. Blues along the top, followed by greens, followed by a row of yellows, all the way down to the reds and blacks at the bottom. I looked on in pride at my handiwork, but instead of that warm feeling welling up inside me, I felt empty.

Then I realized what it was that made the day feel so long. April wasn't in the shop. I'd had to spend shifts in the shop alone, but never with the knowledge that April wasn't going to be in for an entire week.

In fact, before Ethan came into my life again and distracted me, April had already been getting more and more gigs. We never really talked about it but she was going to have enough work soon to not have to work at the shop anymore.

As for myself, I'd avoided thinking about what I'd do when that day came. And now, looking around the empty shop, I wasn't sure *what* I was going to do.

Suddenly, a profound sense of loneliness washed over me.

I went over to the speakers behind the counter, picked up April's pink music player, and turned it on. A catchy tune filled the shop, with Korean vocals I couldn't understand. The beat was exciting and bouncy with the confidence of a bubblegum-chewing teenager with it all figured out. I let the music resonate through my body and get me into a swaying rhythm. There was always something mysteriously delightful about being able to be moved by music even if you couldn't understand the words.

It didn't magically fix everything, but at least the shop didn't feel so lonely anymore.

Running Away

I took an uncharacteristic fourth round through all the closing procedures for the shop tonight, but it still felt like something was off. Humming to myself a loop of three mangled Korean words that had somehow gotten stuck on repeat in the back of my head, I ran my finger down Saturday's to-dos. The list was shorter thanks to a last minute wedding cancellation. The bride-to-be, the bride's maid of honor, as well as the mother-in-law, had all called, each one stating a different reason for the sudden cancellation. I wasn't about to get involved, so I accepted our fees--standard operating procedure--and that was that.

An empty weekend, by myself, no April, and perhaps a good amount of Korean pop music.

Maybe I'll be able to speak Korean by the time I see April again.

I sighed and squashed the urge to make a fifth round of closing checkups.

The backdoor *had* to be locked by now.

I puffed out my chest, grabbed my purse, and walked over to the hooks where I exchanged my work apron for my anorak jacket. It was a ritualistic transition to get myself into the leaving mood. Apron off and jacket on meant I was done for the day. After I straightened my jacket and picked up my purse, I was out on the sidewalk, the shop door making its usual jingling sound behind me.

Outside, it was a clear sky, dark, with a smattering of stars unhindered by the Los Angeles light pollution. A rush of cool night air filled my jacket, causing it to float like a poofy dress as I turned around to lock up the shop. The lock slid into place, and I scanned the shop through the glass, contemplating doing that fifth round afterall.

Actually, was it too late to hit up the climbing wall?

"Sierra."

I spun around, the shop keys falling from my hand, my heart jumping into my throat at the sound of Ethan's voice.

The street lights only lit his face briefly as Ethan stooped down to pick my keys up from the sidewalk.

For a moment, his height and broad shoulders were intimidating in the darkness, an imposing presence within arms reach. Then a warm sensation pulsed throughout my body. Perhaps it was the faint scent of his cologne or the way that he moved, but something about him felt comfortable, familiar, like I was already home. That feeling of comfort brought with it a thought that I'd been suppressing for the past week: I missed him.

"I didn't mean to scare you," Ethan said, handing me the jangling keys, tucking them carefully into my open palm.

"Ethan," I whispered softly, still in disbelief that he was in front of me. He had mentioned that he would be busy with work, so I figured he was back in San Francisco. I was happy to see him but showing up out of the blue without a call or text beforehand was certainly out of the ordinary. Then again, could I really expect ordinary when it came to Ethan Thorne?

It was only after my shock wore off that I noticed something was wrong.

Instead of his hair being tousled in a fashionable way, it was messy, unkempt, and he wore a large bandage on the side of his forehead. My eyes continued taking in his sloppily tucked button down, the smears of dirt all over his outfit, and the sizeable hole at the knee of his khaki pants.

"My gosh, what happened to you?" My voice quivered, my relief at seeing Ethan quickly overcome with worry. I looked around and saw that behind Ethan, was not the black car Manny drove, but a standard taxi, yellow, black lettering, parading a backlit triangular shaped ad on its roof.

"Hm?" Ethan looked at me puzzled. He was wearing a thin sheen of sweat and his stubble had grown longer, a worn five o'clock shadow. He shook his head. "Oh no, nothing, never mind me, I'm fine."

His voice was short and curt and, even though he was looking at me, it felt like he wasn't.

"What's going on?" I asked, trying to straighten out his clothes. "Are you okay?"

I held back on the multitude of questions piling up, waiting on Ethan to say something, *anything*, to explain the state he was in.

"Just business," he replied, dismissively, shuffling his weight from one foot to the other then back again. "Everything will be fine." He rolled up his sleeves and looked at me as if he still hadn't decided which spot on my face to focus on.

It looked like he'd been in some sort of fight but Ethan didn't seem like the type to engage in fisticuffs at the bar. Besides, it was six o'clock in the evening. Or was I to take him at his word that he'd gotten those injuries from work? I knew the upper echelons of business were a boys club, but settling conflicts with a brawl seemed like it'd be going too far.

Whatever had happened, Ethan was clearly shaken.

"Hey," I said firmly, grabbing onto his arm, hoping to pull him back from wherever his mind was. "Just relax." Instead of a barrage of questions, he needed someone to help him cool off. And as much as I wanted answers, I wanted Ethan to be with me, here, grounded in the present.

Ethan started, "I am, it's — "

I stepped in to embrace him, pulling myself into his chest, letting my arms cradle every inch they could. My head rested on his chest, and I could hear his heart thumping, racing, panicked. I closed my eyes and took deep breaths, coaxing Ethan to follow my lead.

Long deep breaths.

A few long seconds later, Ethan brought his arms around me, holding me, his breathing steady. I could already feel his disposition changing, the muscles in his back relaxing, his hold on me calmer, more deliberate, in control.

He was back.

"Sorry," Ethan said with a sigh. "Everything is fine, really." He pulled away from me, hands resting on my shoulders as he gazed at me, his eyes soft. "Let's… Let's go away for a bit."

I took a step back.

"Let's just take a moment," I countered.

"Mm," Ethan nodded at me, his mind busy.

Suddenly, his eyes seemed to snap sharp, aimed right at me, determined. "Let's run away."

I laughed. "Ethan, we need to take a *couple* of steps back. You've just shown up here, you're hurt… Besides what kind of 'business' leads to *this*?" I brought my hand up to the bandage on his head.

Ethan sucked in a breath, looked around the street as if he was just realizing where he was, and let out a sheepish chuckle. "You're right. I'm sorry, this is weird."

"Yes, a little," I agreed, squinting one eye.

"Sometimes my negotiation methods can be unconventional. Risky. Sometimes they work out, other times…" he shrugged, pointing to his head. "I'm fine. Really."

"You're fine?"

"Trust me. Let's get away for the weekend. Just you and me."

Ethan's eyes were twinkling, his usual confidence brimming to the surface, and his smile was back. His warm charming smile, highlighted by those soft lips, close enough to kiss. Heat filled my cheeks and desire pulsed between my legs as my heart pumped fiercely in my chest. Was it possible to want to be even closer to Ethan than I already was? I knew I wanted to be wrapped up in him again, soon.

"Not somewhere far," he added. "I was thinking Vegas? It'll be fun."

I really wanted to accept, but the doubts crept in immediately.

"Vegas? That's still a significant drive, at least—"

"We won't be driving," Ethan interrupted.

"But a flight this last minute? The ticket prices would be insane."

"The plane's already been paid for," Ethan said.

"Oh."

Sometimes I forgot who I was dating and the means he had available.

"So how about it?" he asked.

God knows how lonely I'd been this week, especially with April out. Maybe a fun weekend in Vegas with Ethan was exactly what I needed. There'd be some appointments for the weekend I'd have to rearrange, but nothing that couldn't be pushed off until later in the week. Of course, I didn't fully buy his story about how he'd gotten injured and clearly he wasn't ready to tell me the details yet, but maybe he just needed some time.

Whatever else was going on, from the haunted look in Ethan's eyes, one thing was clear: he needed me.

"I'll have to make some calls," I caught myself saying.

"Fine, fine, I'll be making some myself." His hands squeezed me excitedly.

"And I have to be back Sunday night to be ready for our Monday morning delivery."

"I promise to have you back before curfew," Ethan said with a wink.

"Okay, I'll have to pack and —"

"Now. We have to leave now."

Ethan stared down at me, his expression eerily neutral, but I sensed the returning urgency of earlier, and I could only respond with a nod. It felt right. Taking a spontaneous trip to Vegas was certainly well outside of my comfort zone but I wondered if April would be proud if she saw me now, just going with the flow, trying to see where our adventure would take us.

Sky High

"Happy to see you again so soon, Mr. Thorne!" the pilot announced merrily. "The cleaning crew is still turning over the plane and making sure all the refreshments are fully stocked. They are wrapping up now, and it'll only be a moment. My co-pilot is preparing the plane for take off so we should be able to depart shortly."

Ethan nodded absentmindedly. If they hadn't even turned over his plane yet, then he must've arrived from San Francisco and came to see me immediately. The thought made me feel a mixture of excitement and apprehension. I just hoped that I was up to the task of distracting him from his failed negotiation.

A rushed woman donning an apron hurried down the jet's steps. "Good evening, Mr. Thorne," she said, bowing slightly before attending to her waiting cart, just as a female flight attendant appeared at the entrance of the plane. "We're ready for you," the flight attendant said curtly, smiling to both of us as well as the pilot.

"Please, Mr. Thorne," the pilot said, grandly waving his hand toward the steps of the sleek Gulfstream Jet.

Ethan guided me by the small of my back so that I could board first while he followed behind. When I stepped into the cabin, there was a rush of air, a crisp cool breeze like when you walk into an air conditioned building. My hair flew away from my face, opening my view to the bright interior of the plane.

Instead of a plane's typical fittings of cramped itchy chairs lined up like a school bus, we had practically stepped into a luxury car on steroids. There were large plush beige loungers as well as a couch with all wood trimmings. The flight attendant was standing next to a fully polished oak bar with her hands joined neatly together.

"Sit anywhere you'd like," she said pleasantly, noticing my hesitation.

But I was too busy being awestruck. I know that private jets existed, but to not only see, but set foot in one was quite another thing. I immediately felt self conscious and out of place. If Ethan was surrounded by such luxury on a regular basis, what could I possibly offer him that was sufficiently distracting?

"Why don't you sit over there, Sierra?" Ethan beckoned toward one of the plush chairs facing the back of the plane. Normally, I would have playfully given him a hard time for trying to order me around, but given his fragile state and my awe at the surroundings, I just let it slide and sank into the chair.

It was even softer and more comfortable than it looked.

Ethan sat on the tall lounger diagonally across from me, as if he wanted to keep some distance between us.

Before I could figure out why, the flight attendant interrupted, "Would you like a drink before take off? We carry most types of beverages as well as champagne. I'll be able to serve food when we are at a stable elevation."

"Just water," Ethan said, concentrating on his phone.

Feeling increasingly awkward, I squeaked out a "same for me," sending the flight attendant to the bar as we prepared for take off. It seemed that standard operating procedure was for her to give us a thirty second rundown of the safety precautions and exits of the plane, and then help locate the cleverly tucked away seat belts built into the plush seats. She also informed us that she would remain in the front cabin on the other side of the bar to give us privacy for the duration of the flight.

The pilot announced our departure within a few minutes and we were off the tarmac and into the air in no time at all.

But it gave me enough time to stare at Ethan, wondering what kind of state he was in. I felt certain that he was as glad to see me as I was to see him, but he wasn't showing it in quite the way I might have expected. Was it related to his ruffled condition? He hadn't fully explained and I didn't want to pry if it was something he didn't want to talk about. I was willing to put up with it—for now—but he hadn't even thrown me a bone.

I watched Ethan's face, his determined eyes, his sharp jaw still evident even with the stubble, his muscles around his neck. Then my sights jumped to his hands, those long fingered hands that earnestly searched every inch of me during our first time together. And then to his broad shoulders that had covered me protectively as he cradled me. Need swelled between my legs, sending heat throughout my body, a desperate heat that needed an outlet.

Did he feel the same way? Or was it just me?

Ethan looked preoccupied, his brow furrowed, glancing out the dark window, then back down at his phone.

Ever since we'd stepped on the plane, Ethan had been too in his head to attend to me, forcing me to fend for myself. It was difficult to blame him and I didn't want to be too demanding of his attention but... No, I wasn't quite being honest with myself.

I wanted his attention on me.

I *needed* his attention on me.

When the pilot announced that we were at a stable elevation and could freely walk about the cabin, I immediately unfastened my seatbelt and planted myself next to Ethan.

I could sense Ethan's immediate instinct was to want to scooch over, so I put my hand on his thigh.

Perhaps what we needed was a distraction. Something to make him feel better — to make *me* feel better about having agreed to this trip.

"Are you working on something?" I asked.

"Yeah, let me just finish this." He hadn't bothered looking at me, so I leaned over and started nibbling the bottom of his jaw, letting my tongue trace the bone.

If I wanted a distraction, it'd have to be up to me to make it happen. I was a big girl. I didn't always need to wait for Ethan to initiate.

"Hey, come on," Ethan nudged me away, annoyed. "Later."

I grabbed his face with both hands and covered his protest with my mouth. He tugged away slightly which only got me more riled up. I followed his pull and leaned forward, using the force of my forearms pressing against his chest to lift myself up, straddling him, as I deepened the kiss, forcefully taking what I wanted. It made me feel powerful, like I was conquering a wild animal that could snap and tear me apart at any moment.

Ethan had to gasp for air, torn between whatever was on his phone and the immediate sensations of our lips pressed together.

I leaned back to grind against him, allowing enough space for me to slip my fingers down his shirt to tackle the first shirt button. As I rubbed my heat against his, I could feel Ethan hardening beneath me. Excitement tugged at me hard and I let a small moan slip past my lips.

Ethan suddenly sucked in a sharp breath and grabbed my wrists tightly.

"Sierra, stop."

I pulled against his grip and raised an eyebrow at him.

"Guess you'll just have to stop me then," I replied, swiftly yanking my hands free and grabbing onto his shoulders firmly, using Ethan as a brace to push harder, rub deeper, against his more honest self.

I reached for another kiss, but Ethan turned away, so I landed on his cheek and traced my tongue up to his temple noticing that he was starting to perspire, the heat between us getting to him. His scent was sweet and musky, waking up something primal within me.

I grinned internally and slid a hand up his neck, behind his head, and yanked his hair, pulling his head back in my control as I slammed against him. Harshly taking his mouth right where I wanted him.

Ethan responded instantly.

He grabbed my waist, lifted me easily, and threw me onto the couch. My back slammed against the leather. Then he was on top of me immediately, a tiger jumping on its prey. His breath hitched as he narrowed his eyes down at me, a shared stir of desire between us.

For a long moment, Ethan continued to stare down at me, those fierce eyes, shaded in darkness, finally concentrated on me. Seeing only me.

Looks like I've woken up the kitty cat.

Then Ethan suddenly started pulling back. The loss of sensation of his warmth against me felt like a yawning absence. He'd made his point and was turning away now.

I'd have to make myself clear, offer myself completely to him, so there could be no questions.

I pulled on his shirtsleeve, more gently this time.

"Let me help you...distract you," I said.

Ethan stopped, frozen in place, his gaze intent, his body hovering over me. "Are you certain about this?"

I brushed his fallen hair out of his face, revealing the bandage at his hairline, before letting my fingers graze the thin cut an inch above his jaw, now beginning to scab. "Tell me how you want me."

Ethan sent my wrist slamming back into the leather couch, his grip tightening. He brought his head against mine, inhaling at my neck, lips lingering against my ear. I trembled at his touch, anticipation coursing through my body.

"I want something different," he growled.

Then we were at the back of the plane, Ethan closing the door to the small bedroom cabin luxuriously fitted to comfortably catch some sleep or have some hot breathy fun.

I only had a moment to take in the awe of the cabin before Ethan had me pinned on the bed, both of us sinking into the plush comforter. He appeared to measure my body with his eyes, lids drooping slightly, his expression shifting. I pulled his face close, and his lips pressed then parted my own, his tongue reaching in, engulfing me, enjoying the search for my hot spots.

Ethan lifted himself away to search for something in a nearby drawer, and then turned back to me. The dark intensity of his eyes, the fire behind them, was the last thing I saw before Ethan slipped the sleeping mask over my head and I was left in darkness.

I instinctively lifted my hands to it.

"Don't," Ethan grunted, the command freezing me, sending a shiver up my spine, the vibrations tingling, my heart racing.

I felt the bed shift, Ethan resting on his knees, the sound of him unbuckling his belt and pulling that leather straight off, smoothly through the belt loops. I gasped in surprise as he seized both my hands, sending them above my head and tying his belt around my wrists securing them together and around what must have been a hidden seat belt.

Ethan tightened the knot, the leather pinching into my skin, and I winced, unable to hold back a soft struggling whine.

"That'll only provoke me," he hummed in a low voice, dripping with hunger.

Being blind to Ethan's face, his movements, his intentions, I grew more aware of my other senses as my anticipation grew. The hum of the plane muffled all other sounds and the recycled air left a staleness to most smells, but with Ethan on top of me, the deadened sounds and smells blended together, a dull backdrop to music of Ethan's steady breathing and the woody citrus smell of his cologne. All my senses were not only surrounded by Ethan, but seeking him out, searching for more.

His head lowered to mine, his hair brushing against my cheek, as he trailed kisses down my neck. Those soft lips found a spot close to my collarbone that it liked and nibbled gently as Ethan's hands found their way under my shirt, slightly rough fingers sliding up my torso, pulling my shirt up along with them.

I felt a sharp bite and reflexively pulled away, tugging against the belt restraining my arms.

A quick jolt of fear shot through me at the sharp pain as well as the reminder of the restraint on my wrists. I had wanted this, but the unpredictability made me feel like every hair on my body was standing, alert, afraid, and anxious.

Ethan's reaction was swift, yanking both my shirt and bra all the way up to reveal my breasts. His coarse hands grabbed and held my waist down, jamming my lower back into the bed, then I felt his tongue at my nipple in slow wet circular motions.

"Ethan," I moaned as he devoured me, his grip at my waist tightened.

I felt another sharp bite at the inside of one of my breasts.

"Ouch!" I yelped, tugging again at the restraint, wriggling uselessly under Ethan's muscled hands, an immovable strength.

"Is that a complaint?" Ethan's voice vibrated against my body.

A whimper of desire escaped me as his stiff member pressed against my crotch, rubbing my heat through my pants, the hard mass unmistakable.

Then he was unzipping and pulling my pants and panties down to my ankles. I expected him to remove my shoes and the rest, but instead, he positioned himself between my legs my pants acting at an additional restraint on my ankles. I was forced to spread my knees apart to accommodate his torso. Thankful to be blinded, embarrassment beat in my chest at displaying myself for Ethan.

He pushed my thighs wider, then higher, and I released a throaty gasp as his hand cupped against me, covering me as if to keep my urge from exploding, but instead, it only prevented the heat from escaping, building the intensity.

His mouth came down to capture mine, taking the opening of my gasp to enter and plunder. My mind was overwhelmed. The sensations were too intense and too numerous for me to concentrate on any single one. I could only relinquish myself to both our desires.

Then Ethan maneuvered lower, his silky shirt brushing my bare legs, a reminder that I was the only one exposed. His steamy breath at my needy entrance sent a shiver up my spine. My heart pounded, unsure of Ethan's expression, but very aware of his labored breathing as he observed me.

"Tell me what you want," he said, an edge to his voice betraying his own craving.

Something pressed my clit and I could only gasp, "More."

I squeezed my eyes shut at the sudden harsh pinch of another bite from Ethan, this time at my inner thigh.

Then his finger was inside me. First one, testing out the waters to quickly discover that I was ready for more, then two, as Ethan impaled me.

I tried to spread my legs wider, opening myself up to him.

"How bad do you want to come?" he breathed.

I managed a choked moan as Ethan's mouth came down to join his fingers.

My ears filled with my own uncontrollable sounds. My heart felt like it was beating too hard. I panted and shuddered, my body demanding release, as I managed to grip the sheets where my hands were bound, wringing them between my fingers. I arched my back as the excitement between my legs came bearing down like an approaching train.

Then it was gone without ever arriving, suddenly, light blinding me, the mask coming off. My eyes immediately blinked shut, then slowly opened to see Ethan.

He was standing next to the bed looking down at me.

His hooded eyes, dark and piercing. Beads of sweat on his brow, and a prominent vein on his throat.

I could almost see his ragged breath in the air.

I started to say something, but stopped when Ethan narrowed his gaze.

"I want you to wait," he said. "Wait for me."

Tease

My mind was a haze as we made our way to a waiting towncar and then to the Vegas strip. I could vaguely remember the tall buildings and lights emerging from the desert, until we were in the middle of it all, the honks of the cars around us, the throngs of walking tourists, the yelling sales people and hawkers enthusiastically handing out cards and flyers.

I was still reeling from the game that Ethan was playing with me.

I had to keep my eyes focused on the sights outside the car window because I knew that even looking at Ethan would make me lose my mind. The most I saw was the corner of his dark navy slacks and brown shoes, a new suit that had been conveniently waiting for him in the narrow closet of the plane.

Ethan was acting like he was in a library, all tight and quiet. I hadn't felt him budge even in the slightest on the other side of the car's leather seat.

The sweat began to bead at the back of my neck as I realized that I was constantly switching my legs, crossing the left over the right, then the right over the left, my elevated foot kicking the air impatiently.

"How about we stop by a place to get you clothes and the things you'll need for the weekend?" Ethan asked, his voice cool and collected, like he was just asking me if I wanted some tea.

Was he serious right now?

We were both horny out of our minds, and he wanted to delay our gratification for some essentials? I knew I needed clothes, and well, all those other things, but I almost screamed that it was the last thing I *really* needed.

But no, this was Ethan's game, and he wanted me to wait.

So I *would* wait.

Because I *could* play this game.

I cleared my throat, delivering a very casual, "That's a great idea, thank you."

Patience wasn't exactly my strong suit, but I could hold out for a while longer.

We were dropped off at a large glass-doored entrance, and upon stepping inside, a welcome breeze of cool air rushed out from inside the building. A light floral scent filled the air and the decor trended modern with lots of metal accents. There were escalators and multiple floors full of boutiques, and the eye-catching marvelous architecture pieces elevated the shopping experience. I could tell that all the stores had to be very high end because I couldn't recognize practically any of the brands, and the place was surprisingly empty. I had no idea what most of the stores sold, but they must've been expensive.

I would have felt very awkward and plain and ordinary if I hadn't been devoting every ounce of energy to ignoring the need between my legs.

Thankfully, Ethan quickly led us to one boutique. The sales person instantly recognized Ethan, and we were escorted deeper into the store.

"Will this be for yourself, Mr. Thorne? Or for your lovely guest?" The suited woman smiled pleasantly to the both of us, and a suited man, standing by the checkout desk, stopped what he was doing to smile and deliver a small bow in greeting.

"For both of us," Ethan replied. "I'll have the usual pieces for the weekend, both casual and formal events. The same for my guest."

The sales woman nodded to the man who swiftly left the desk, pulling a rack on wheels from the back.

"We will prepare some options for your companion while we select your suits, Mr. Thorne." She showed us to the opulent dressing room, that had two heavily curtained fitting stalls with a plush circular couch in the center. It looked like the celebrity closets I'd see on TV.

The woman motioned elegantly to one of the stalls which, upon closer inspection as I stepped inside, was more generously sized than it first appeared.

I heard the curtain swish closed behind me and turned around a bit startled.

"Excellent timing," the woman said. I heard the sound of wheels on plush carpet and the rustling of clothes on a hanger. "The assortment of clothes and accessories are grouped from casual to formal. Various shoes are arranged in the same order at the back of the fitting stall next to the mirror. My name is Sara, please call for me if you require assistance."

The loud swish of hooks on a metal rod was followed by silence.

I peeked out of the dressing room to see the large rack of clothing within arms reach. There were both loud and soft colors, sequins and shimmery gowns, and an array of shoes and purses, as well as a standing tray with jewelry.

Ethan was seated on the circular couch looking at his phone. Now that the employees were gone, I could finally focus on what I really wanted. Ethan Thorne's body.

My eyes crawled up his long legs, to his straight torso, then to his jawline softened by that five o'clock shadow. My focus centered on his lips. That mouth had been doing amazing things just moments ago.

Ethan suddenly interrupted.

"Two each of a casual, semi-formal, and formal will be sufficient. Pick what you like."

He kept his eyes attached to his phone.

I checked Ethan's crotch to see if he had a boner, but if he had one, I couldn't see it. How could he keep himself under such iron self-control? I was almost certain that he was more than feeling it too on the plane. It wasn't just me.

But I wasn't a hundred percent sure, and I was feeling too impatient to keep still and actually think, so I figured my best course of action was to hurry with the clothes and get to the hotel as soon as possible. The faster the better so that we could finish what we'd started on the plane.

I grabbed the first group of clothing in one big armful and skillfully hung them inside the dressing room. I was both impressed and a bit embarrassed that the saleswoman had guessed my size so accurately. My clothes hit the floor faster than an apple falling from a tree as I shimmied into each of the outfits, quickly narrowing down the options, then moving on to the next group of clothing before getting to the last and final group.

Slipping on the first cocktail dress, I frowned at discovering that I couldn't reach the zipper. So much for getting out of here quickly.

Leaving the dress only partially zipped, I poked my head out to find Ethan, who hadn't moved an inch, phone still in hand in the exact same position.

"Ethan," I started. "Can you help me zip this? I can't get a good idea of the fit without it zipped all the way up."

Ethan seemed to sink into the couch, as he stayed frozen a beat longer than I'd expected, before putting his phone into his jacket's inner pocket and standing up. His gaze seemed to look past me as he steadily walked over.

I turned so that he could assist me, pulling my hair out of the way, and I felt Ethan pinch the fabric of the dress away from my body and heard the zipper travel up. He had managed to zip the thing without me feeling his touch at all.

But I felt his breath at my shoulder, a hot sensation, a pant of desire. I noticed Ethan leaning in a bit and, thinking he was going to kiss me, turned to meet him, but his head snapped away following the zipper instead.

"Do you need me to help unzip the dress as well?"

"U-um," I stuttered. I quickly turned to the mirror to see that I didn't really like the dress. "Yes, if you would."

I turned around again, lifted my hair again, and Ethan again skillfully unzipped the dress a little below the spot the zipper had been when I had first asked for his help.

"Thank you," I said, letting my hair fall back down.

From the reflection in the mirror I first noticed Ethan's hand traveling along the edge of the curtain to pull it closed, then quickly caught his eyes from over my shoulder.

He was staring at me.

Ethan's dark eyes were piercing, narrowed, his brows hooded, shading them. They lingered for a moment before the curtain swung shut.

So much for cool, calm, and collected. The great Ethan Thorne had made a mistake. He'd caught me off guard on the plane, but perhaps he needed to feel the heat of the challenge as well.

A smirk spread across my face as I felt my blood pumping through me, my heart pounding through my ears.

Now it was my turn.

I donned a slim, glove-like, dress and carefully selected the most strappy complicated heels, then yanked the curtains open.

Ethan flinched just slightly, but kept his cool.

"Could you help me put these shoes on? I want to see them with this dress, but the dress is rather constricting."

I sat on the ottoman inside the dressing room and Ethan walked over, then bent on one knee next to me as he handled the left heel first.

"I just need help with the straps," I said, slipping my left foot into the skinny heel. "Here, let me get comfortable." I scooched my foot closer to Ethan, then lifted my right foot onto his knee.

Ethan concentrated on getting the straps on, buckling and wrapping, and I slowly leaned forward, letting my right foot slide along his inner thigh.

"There, it's done," Ethan said, about to turn to pick up the matching heel.

"No," I interrupted curtly. "The straps are wrong. You have to wrap it around the back of my ankle first."

Ethan raised his eyebrow. "Why didn't you—"

The balls of my right foot pressed his crotch, and rubbed against something very hard and excited.

Ethan shot to his feet. "Sierra."

"I just wanted some help," I said innocently, like I didn't notice the rising tent in his slacks. "Fine fine, I'll do it myself. The dress is just in the way." I stood, turning toward the mirror, hiking the dress all the way up to the bottom of my butt, before bending over to fix the straps of the shoe.

I was only halfway down to touching the straps when Ethan grabbed me from behind, pressing my arms, squeezing them against my torso, and shoving me against the adjacent wall of the dressing room.

I smiled internally, that'd certainly gotten a rise out of him.

His chest pushed into my back and I gasped a choked moan as Ethan pressed his hard cock against my now exposed butt, separated by the thin fabric of his pants.

"You're not wearing anything," he growled, both angry and lustful.

"Just the dress," I whispered. "For now."

Ethan grunted, then grinded harder into me, his teeth biting at my neck. He grabbed my hips, and I bit my lip in anticipation when he briefly lifted me but ultimately dropped me back onto the ottoman.

My eyes flicked in shock up at him.

Ethan's face was flushed, sweating.

"No," he said simply.

He turned on his heel, leaving, tearing the curtains closed.

That definitely counted as a win for me.

April had been right all along, the ribbon that Ethan had so gently wrapped around my ankle and tied into a bow had had sexual intention behind it. He'd always wanted to bind my sexuality, tease it, play with it, control it.

The first night we'd met, we'd both been angling to control the situation, gain an upper hand. Yet, we'd been playing the game under different rules, mismatched and out of sync.

Now, things had changed between us. We'd seen each other behind our masks, but we were still playing out the very same game.

The stakes were higher — our true selves on the line — but I was no longer afraid to play. In fact, I looked forward to the challenge, even relished it. Ethan had showed me how to enjoy the delicious pressure building inside me, the crackling sexual tension held between us.

Later, in the silent hours of the night, as I drifted off into fevered dreams, I wondered which of us would lose control first? Ethan or I?

Mr. Thorne will return...

...but if you can't *wait*

...then sign up for my mailing list at
http://lkrayne.com
to receive **Thorne Two**,
an EXCLUSIVE chapter from Mr.
Thorne's perspective.

This bonus will NOT be available
anywhere else...

Dear Lovely Reader,

Thank you so much for reading Satin & Thorne! I've certainly had a blast writing this story and I'm overjoyed that it is finally in your hands.

Stories are my favorite way to connect with people, but sometimes writing a book can feel like a lonely road with sparse feedback along the way.

After the publication of Satin & Thorne, I've been delighted to find that one of the greatest joys of this process has been seeing reviews from readers like yourself. If you loved this story, I'd love to hear about it! What was your favorite scene? Maybe a favorite moment?

Again, thank you so much for taking the time to read my book. There are an endless number of books to choose from, so as an author just starting out, I truly appreciate you giving me a chance! :)

Cheers,
Liv

Mr. Thorne appears in the Silk & Thorne Trilogy:

Silk & Thorne

Satin & Thorne

Lace & Thorne

Lace & Thorne (Silk & Thorne 3)

Las Vegas. City of Dreams, City of Sin. The cat and mouse game between Ethan Thorne and I led us to this place of lights and glitter. Here, our relationship would enter a new phase as a high stakes game of poker provokes a side of Ethan that I'd never seen before.

But secrets cannot be hidden forever. In the glitzy VIP backrooms of the Las Vegas Strip, Ethan puts everything he's ever built on the line as he reveals his true self: a reckless gambler, hurtling toward oblivion.

Out of my element and reeling from the revelation, I place my bets and I play my hand. But all actions have consequences and my desperate moves bring our game to his boardroom. With suited saboteurs around every corner, and Ethan's betrayal still fresh, will we ever find out what was true and good between us or will our masks destroy us both?

Perhaps, as it always had been, the truth could only be found in the past…

In Upstate New York, during that one hot summer, spent amongst the oaks and cicadas…

Sierra and Ethan return to where it all began in this final installment of the Silk & Thorne series.

Keep reading for an exclusive excerpt
from Lace & Thorne (Silk & Thorne 3)…

Ethan and I walked through the service corridors of the Bellagio in tense silence, passing by blank doors leading to unknown parts of the casino. Other than the occasional employee — who paid us no mind in our formal wear — the hallways were empty.

The only sounds I could hear were my heartbeat thudding in my chest and the clack of my heels echoing off the walls.

Ethan pulled me along, his hand gripping mine firmly. I could tell his mouth was in a thin line from the brief glimpses I snuck.

He clearly wasn't pleased.

Good, that made two of us.

My face felt flushed, whether from the exertion of trying to keep up with Ethan, or excitement from winning the poker game, I couldn't tell.

There was a needy, desperate energy building in my sex. It was an inappropriate time for it, and at first I thought it was from the fact that I'd yet to have an orgasm, despite our sexually charged evening, but for some reason the feeling only grew as I watched Ethan stalk angrily down the corridor ahead of me.

A disturbing thought broke into my consciousness.

Was I the instigator? Purposefully prodding at Ethan until he snapped? Was I trying to escalate some unspoken game between us? To see who could wait longer? To see who had more self control? To tempt him to lose it and punish me?

Images of my wrists looped in a rough leather belt, my arms over my head, my legs spread wide for Ethan's glistening body flashed through my mind.

The fantasies disturbed me, turning me on, yet further fanning the flames of anger in my chest. I'd trusted Ethan enough to fly with him to Vegas. I'd participated willingly in the games and teasing, I'd given him something of myself, something I was terrified of exposing, yet when it came down to it, he valued his poker game over my needs.

My steps slowed and Ethan—still walking—jerked my arm from the momentum before spinning around.

I planted my feet, prying Ethan's strong fingers off of my hand.

"I'm done," I said. "I'm not taking another step."

Ethan let my hand fall away, and bore down on me, his imposing chest towering toward me.

"What the fuck was that?" he growled.

"What the fuck was *what?*" I snapped back.

"Did you consider what might have happened had you lost?"

I knew the words were only going to make things worse as they came out of my mouth, but I couldn't help myself, I'd bit back too much already.

"What's the big deal?" I asked. "You said I could gamble with your card."

"Damn it, Sierra." Ethan ran his hand through his hair, grasping his locks in frustration. "You don't know what these people are like."

"I have a pretty good idea," I said. "High stakes gambling, no consideration for others, seems like you'd fit right in."

"That's not—" Ethan closed his eyes, taking a few deep breaths. "You shouldn't have drawn attention to yourself. You shouldn't have even spoken to him."

Something in me snapped.

I jabbed a finger into Ethan's chest, hard. "You don't get to tell me what to do," I said, my voice rising. "I'm not your corsage and I'm not your goddamn trophy!"

At the far end of the hall, an employee dressed in a black vest and white shirt stopped to watch us curiously, but I was far too angry to care.

Ethan turned to see what I was looking at. Then he shook his head, moving in closer to me, reaching for my arm.

"I was just trying to protect you," he said in a pacifying tone, trying to calm me down. But I didn't want to be calmed down by the great Ethan Thorne.

"Real nice job, bringing me to that charming little venue. Is that your idea of protecting me?" I reached into my purse and pulled out a handful of the stock certificates that the dealer had handed me when Ethan dragged me out of the Black Diamond.

Ethan put a finger to his lips. "Please, you're making a scene."

"Is this your idea of protecting me too?" I said, waving the certificates at him, practically shouting. "What, so you can take whatever risks you like, but I need to be *protected* the minute I'm—"

Before I could react, Ethan grabbed my shoulders and pushed me through a small doorway, slamming the door shut behind us. Suddenly, I was nearly chest to chest with him, breathing hard. His face was just inches from mine. His eyes were glistening and wild.

It took a moment for me to notice the shelves behind Ethan's head. They were stacked full of paper towels, cleaning liquid in spray bottles, and boxes of unopened trash bags.

There was barely enough room for the two of us to fit inside the tiny supply closet, much less with the full weight of our emotions crammed in there with us. The air was thick and suffocating. I felt like I couldn't breath. If I didn't leave I'd blow up, right then and there.

I reached for the door, but Ethan shifted to the left, blocking me in.

"Let's sort this out," he said, crossing his arms stubbornly.

A dull drumbeat throbbed in my temples and I suppressed a scream.

"Fine, you want to talk? Let's talk. I agreed to this trip to Vegas to spend some time with you, not to watch you have some chest thumping display with some rich asshole."

"That's not what that was," Ethan insisted.

"Then what was it?"

I waited patiently as Ethan struggled to find the words, his jaw working.

"Spare me the bullshit. You don't need to tell me everything Ethan, but I draw the line at when you send me away to play with your stupid money, like I'm some sort of *whore*."

Ethan slammed his fist on the shelf behind me, a loud clang ringing in the tight space. "That's not what I meant."

"Then what did you mean?" I asked, eyes narrowed.

Ethan sucked in a deep breath and raised his gaze to the ceiling, but he didn't answer that question either.

Even if I wanted to give him the benefit of the doubt, he was making it exceedingly difficult. I turned around so I wouldn't have to watch him. We'd kicked this whole thing off with aliases, lies, and games. Who were we to think that it would end any different from how it started?

"It was all just a game to you wasn't it?" I asked, my voice cracking slightly. "Teasing me, tempting me, making me wait, not letting me come. You just wanted me to be desperate for your attention, to crave your touch?"

Lace & Thorne (Silk & Thorne 3)

Copyright © 2019 by 1907 Publishing LLC

All rights reserved. No part of this publication may be reproduced, distributed, or transmitted in any form or by any means, including photocopying, recording, or other electronic or mechanical methods, without the prior written permission of the publisher, except in the case of brief quotations embodied in critical reviews and certain other noncommercial uses permitted by copyright law.

Copyright © 2019 by 1907 Publishing LLC

All characters appearing in this work are fictitious. Any resemblance to real persons, living or dead, is purely coincidental.

Printed in Great Britain
by Amazon

46086803R00128